The Reluctant Governess

A Phaeton Regency Romance

by
Pamela Cleaver

ISBN: 1-58749-530-9

Earthling Press ~ United States of America

The Reluctant Governess by Pamela Cleaver
Copyright 2003, 2004, 2005

Print edition 2004
ISBN: 1-58749-530-9

Electronic edition 2004
ISBN: 1-58749-397-7
All trade paperback and electronic rights reserved

www.awe-struck.net

This is work of fiction. People and locations, even those with real names, have been fictionalized for the purpose of this story.

Published by Earthling Press, a subsidiary of Awe-Struck E-Books, Inc.

Available in electronic formats and in print

Editors: Kathryn Struck and Dick Claassen

Prologue

It was high tide and the night was as black as the devil's waistcoat. On the beach, pinpoints of light made by carefully shaded lanterns moved stealthily. Although the area was crowded, the men were as disciplined and orderly as King George's troops. The loudest noise was the sea sucking at the shingle as it moved restlessly.

Jem, the blacksmith, stood directing the operation as ankers of spirits, chests of tea and parcels of tobacco were transferred from the dinghies along a human chain to the line of ponies waiting patiently on the dunes above the beach.

A man in one of the boats spoke to the burly smith. "Alors, mon ami, zat is all. And the money?"

Jem, sinister in the shadows cast by the lantern he held aloft, told the boatman to wait. He walked up the line of porters, past the pack ponies to a figure that stood among the dunes watching. It was a tall man muffled in a caped topcoat, a tricorne pulled down to shade his eyes and the lower part of his face obscured by a dark bandanna.

The blacksmith touched his forehead. "All done, sir. The Frenchie wants his pay."

The man produced a heavy wash leather bag. "What about the silk and lace, Jem? Get that before you pay him and bring it to me."

The blacksmith nodded and took the bag of guineas down to the dinghy, wading out to speak to the Frenchman. After a low voiced conversation, he exchanged the gold for a neat parcel wrapped in oiled silk, tied with tape and sealed with wax. He took it ashore and gave it to the waiting man.

"Right Jem, that's my share." He handed the smith a smaller bag. "Stow the goods and pay the men."

As he strode off into the night, one of the smugglers who by day was a fisherman whispered to Jem in his rich, Suffolk accent, "Who do he be, bor?"

"You know better'n ask that, Bill. Them that asks no questions isn't told no lies. He be the guv'nor, the Master-smuggler. It ain't healthy to know his name."

Bill spoke nervously. "Only joshing, Jem. That do be no business of mine. He could be Black Shuck hisself for all I care so long as I gets my guinea for my night's work."

"Do you keep it like that, bor."

Jem smiled to himself. Of all the men on the beach, only he knew the name of the Master-smuggler.

Chapter One

She was not going to cry, she must be brave. But in spite of her resolve, Belinda's body drooped as she sat on the bed in Aunt Henshaw's tiny guest room. Her dark curls fell forward onto her pale cheeks and her grey eyes were full of unshed tears as she bent over the letter. She read it again, hoping it would mean something different this time.

Spain, 1811.

Dear Miss Farrington,
It is my painful duty to convey sad tidings to you. Recently a battle took place which was, thank God, a victory for our army.
Although our regiment was not involved in the fighting, we helped afterwards to succour the fallen. While we were moving the wounded, Lieutenant George Parker was killed by a sniper's bullet.
Please believe me, dear Miss Farrington, when I assure you it was a clean death. Your fiancé was killed instantly and did not suffer.
I beg you will accept my condolences and those of George's brother officers. He will be sorely missed by us but, I know, even more by you. He seldom talked of aught else but his dear Belinda.
With my sincere sympathy.

...and it was signed by George's colonel.
Belinda was glad to know that she had been so much in George's thoughts. She shrank from picturing him dead on a battlefield, preferring to remember him as she had first seen him at the Harrogate Assembly Rooms, a handsome, romantic figure, tall and elegant in his rifle-green regimentals.

Belinda, fresh from the schoolroom, found him dazzling and godlike. When he asked her to dance, she had been so enthralled, she almost swooned. As he talked, she found they had many tastes in common and quickly she fell deliciously and deliriously in love.

Papa had approved of George and gave him permission to make Belinda an offer and they became engaged just before George received his orders to join his regiment. Their whirlwind courtship was entirely to her taste, matching exactly the adventures of heroines in the marble-covered novels she loved to read.

She sighed. Those were the days: Mamma and Papa had been alive then. How she wished for her parents now: what a comfort Mamma's sympathetic shoulder would have been, what solace to have heard Papa's words of consolation. All the people she loved best had deserted her—Mamma, Papa and George. She was a penniless, homeless orphan without prospects of marriage. Where could she go? How would she live? It was enough to make anyone cry.

When Papa, then Mamma died, Aunt Henshaw came briskly to her rescue. "Well, darling girl, you cannot stay here at the parsonage," she said bracingly. "A new incumbent will be here before we have time to turn round. Life must go on."

She helped Belinda sell the furniture from the house; she helped Belinda pack her possessions then took her to her house in Harrogate where Belinda had been living ever since, waiting for George's return from the wars. Now, he too was dead and with him, all her bright dreams for the future were gone.

Belinda wondered what the heroine of one of her favourite three-decker romances would do in such circumstances? Belinda rather thought she would clutch her head and say, "All is finished!" and go into a decline. But Belinda was too much Papa's daughter and too much a Yorkshire woman with all that county's bluntness, to see herself dying of a broken heart however sad it was to have lost George.

Fetching a handkerchief from her dresser drawer, she wiped her eyes and blew her nose. She knew Papa would have deplored her self-pity.

"Nothing is more tiresome than a woman who bemoans her fate," he used to say.

The Reverend Tertius Farrington, the third son of old Lord Farlow, had been a sensible man who cared for his flock well, but his passion and his downfall had been hunting. A bruising rider to hounds, he broke his neck attempting an impossible fence.

Belinda mourned him sincerely, she had been very close to him. He had delighted in her company and had enjoyed reading history with her to supplement her governess's instruction and to counteract her taste for lurid romances. He frequently shook his head over her addiction to the contents of the circulating library.

"The writers of romances are the greatest enemies of truth and sober sense," he would say, but softened his severity with an affectionate smile.

He had been more severe about her tendency to jump to conclusions and thereby make false judgements, prophesying that it would land her in trouble one day.

She asked her mother about this.

"It is not important for ladies to make judgements, dear," Selina Farrington replied. "When they are young, their fathers tell them what to think and when they are married, they turn to their husbands."

Belinda thought this attitude mealy-mouthed but then, Belinda was spirited unlike Mrs. Farrington who was a gentle, adoring wife. Upon her husband's death, she went into a decline and followed him to the grave six weeks later.

In spite of these two devastating blows, Belinda managed to behave reasonably and had come about. She had great resilience like her aunt Letitia Henshaw, Mamma's widowed sister, a lady with backbone who was quite capable of forming her own opinions and looking after herself.

Aunt Henshaw! Belinda gave a guilty start. She ought to be helping her, not moping. She owed her aunt any service she could perform in return for her kindness and hospitality.

Before going downstairs, Belinda bathed her eyes and tied her dark curls up on the crown of her head with a black ribbon. She smoothed the grey poplin of her high-waisted round dress; she was still in half-mourning for her parents. Now she would have to go into dreary black again for George. She sighed and went downstairs.

* * *

Aunt Henshaw's tiny home was like a dolls' house and the small rooms were crammed with a profusion of old-fashioned furniture. Belinda found her aunt in the parlour dusting and arranging her best china which was kept in a glass fronted cabinet.

Letty Henshaw was a small woman who had become plump with middle age.

"Modern fashions make women my shape look like pillows tied up with string,"she had pronounced. Consequently she scorned the narrow, high-waisted dresses of the day, preferring the flowing loose-backed gowns of her youth. When Belinda found her, she was wearing a snuff coloured brocade saque with an apron tied over it. A lawn cap was perched on her head at a rakish angle and there was a smudge of dust on her right cheek. The effect was comical but Belinda was used to her aunt's eccentric appearance and did not regard it.

"There you are, darling girl." Her aunt greeted Belinda with a cheerful smile. "Just in time to help with the Spode and Rockingham. I daren't trust it to Betsy. Most maids are clumsy but she is the outside of everything, the stoutest things come to pieces in her hands."

"I'm sorry I was so long, Aunt, I was reading that letter again."

"Not moping, were you? I know you have suffered three severe blows in the past year, but you must resist the temptation to behave like a tragedy queen. Turn your thoughts to the present." Aunt Henshaw handed her a soft cloth and a piece of china. "Don't think about the past."

Belinda thought it a little unfair to be called a tragedy queen when she was trying to be brave and sensible. She sniffed, hoping tears would not come, and began to dust the china basket.

"I must not only think about the present, Aunt," she said with resolution, "I need to think about my future. I should like to discuss it with you."

"What is there to talk about, my love? You may not have parents or a fiancé but you are not alone in the world. You will stay here with me."

"I cannot do that—'t'would be an imposition. It has been a squeeze for two of us living in your dear little house that was only meant for one. I am grateful for its shelter and although we have managed perfectly so far, it would not do as a permanent arrangement."

Belinda put it tactfully, but after the airy spaces of the rambling parsonage she was finding the cramped conditions stifling. Besides, she did not want to go on living in Harrogate, it was too full of memories. Every time she went shopping for her aunt, she recalled expeditions with Mamma. If they went for a drive, Belinda was reminded of visiting parishioners with Papa. Even going to the circulating library made her think of Papa's laughter at her shudders over The Mystery of Udolpho. As for going to the Assembly Rooms: she was sure she could never go there again without tearfully remembering dancing romantically with poor George.

"Perhaps you need a change of air. You could go away for a visit. Why do you not get in touch with your papa's elder brother? You might enjoy Farlow Court."

Belinda shook her head. "He and Papa quarrelled, Aunt. I could no more live on Lord Farlow's charity than I can be a burden to you. I must find something to fill my days and provide me with an income."

Aunt Henshaw handed her another piece of china.

"That is easier said than done, my pet. There are few occupations open to young females of gentle birth."

There was a scheme in Belinda's mind which she had long cherished. It had not seemed possible before, but perhaps now that her circumstances had changed, this was the moment to expose it to another's eyes.

"Perhaps I could write romances for a living," she suggested tentatively.

Aunt Henshaw shook her head so vigourously that her lawn cap was in danger of falling off.

"Don't place any hopes in that direction! A girl of eighteen with no experience of life who has never been outside Yorkshire has nothing to say that the world wants to hear. You may have read a quantity of books but what you find easy to read would prove difficult to write."

"You are probably right." Belinda sighed: she was a little crestfallen as her treasured dream met with opposition. "In that case, Aunt, there is no other course open to me than to find a rich old gentleman who is come to Harrogate to drink the waters and marry him." There was an irrepressible twinkle in her eye.

Letty Henshaw nearly dropped the figurine she was dusting.

"Belinda! Don't say such a shocking thing. How could you?"

"Only funning, Aunt, I didn't really mean it."

"I should hope not indeed. It was a jest in poor taste. It quite upset me."

Belinda tried her last throw. She had been thinking hard and although the idea was not very appealing, it would gain her a measure of independence which she felt she sorely needed.

"There is one other thing I have thought of," said Belinda

industriously cleaning the crevices of a statuette. "Perhaps I could be a governess."

Aunt Henshaw sniffed but this time she didn't look as if she were about to have palpitations. She handed Belinda a tureen shaped like a cabbage.

"That is certainly more eligible than your earlier suggestions which were quite frivolous. But have you really considered what it would mean? Governesses lead sadly dreary lives, looked down upon by family and servants alike."

"It need not be so. My own governess, Mademoiselle Berlemont, had a pleasant life in our household. She was treated more as if she were an elder sister than a governess. She was as well-born as I am; she was a refugee from the revolution in France while I am a genteel orphan."

"I suppose it would be possible. You are certainly well-informed and your needlework leaves nothing to be desired," Aunt Henshaw allowed.

"My sketching and water colouring are adequate and as I always spoke French with Ma'm'selle, I am perfectly at home in that tongue," added Belinda. "I have always heard that competence in French is a trump card for a governess."

"I cannot like it. You are too young, darling, to devote yourself to such a course. Might you not meet an eligible young man and fall in love?" she asked wistfully.

"How can you say so?" Belinda's eyes clouded. "Who could compare with George? And who would take me without a dowry? Now that Papa's debts are paid, I have no more than enough to keep me clad."

Letitia Henshaw sighed again. "A penniless gentle-woman is much to be pitied. I suppose you might be a governess, but Belinda dear, you have no experience of children to recommend you; not even helping with brothers and sisters."

"That is true but I remember what it was like to be a child and I like the little creatures. It cannot be so very difficult to look after one or two little girls and perhaps a little boy."

As Aunt Henshaw was childless and Belinda an only child,

neither of them realised the enormity of this optimistic notion. So as her aunt did not oppose it, albeit she was not enthusiastic, Belinda considered the matter settled.

"Advise me, Aunt, how shall I go about finding a situation?"

"If that is what you are determined to do, we will make enquiries. I shall ask among my friends and we will look at advertisements in the journals. But don't leave me just yet, my dear, let us spend Christmas together; it will be time enough in the spring."

Belinda agreed. Having dealt with two sad losses in her life already that year, she knew she needed time to grieve for George before she began a new life.

* * *

That year in Yorkshire, it began to snow before Christmas. Day after day, huge flakes like goose down from a split pillow fell, blanketing the two villages that together made up the spa of Harrogate. Fortunately, Aunt Henshaw's little house was in High Harrogate near the shops and the circulating library so, although cut off from the rest of the county by drifts, they were able to procure the necessities of life.

Christmas was kept quietly out of respect for Belinda's mourning. Her aunt treated her with kindness but she had little sympathy with Belinda's occasional bouts of dramatic self-pity when Belinda behaved in the manner her aunt disparagingly referred to as her tragedy queen act. Whenever such tendencies came upon her niece, she told her sharply not to put on airs, to be interesting and set her tasks such as keeping her wardrobe in repair and mending household linen. Occasionally the monotony of their life was lifted when Aunt Henshaw's friends came to tea or when they played cards, but it was hardly an exciting life for a girl of eighteen.

Gradually Belinda began to feel as if she were suffocating,

she began to chafe against the bonds of imprisonment imposed by her mourning. As the snow melted and the days lengthened, snowdrops and crocuses struggled up through the chilly earth. As if she too were affected by the season's renewal, Belinda began to come to life.

At last a day came when she threw her sewing aside.

"I'm sick of wearing the willow," she cried with her old spirit. "I'm tired of black dresses and bonnets. I want to dance, to go to the theatre, and talk with people my own age. It is a shocking thing to say, Aunt, but I confess I'm tired of mourning George."

Aunt Henshaw was not shocked. She got up from her chair and ran to embrace her niece.

"Darling child, at last you are cured! I never said so to you or to your poor, dear, unworldly mamma, but I knew from the first that what you felt for George was not true love."

Belinda looked questioningly at her aunt's plump, beaming face. "Not true love?" she said in surprise.

"You were so young when you met him, darling, straight from the schoolroom and your head was full of love stories. Of course you were going to think yourself in love with the first handsome man in uniform who paid you compliments and told you that you were pretty. You were in love with the idea of love. George Parker, on the other hand, was in love with himself—I saw it at once. He was delighted to find a sweet little girl to worship him and when he saw your mamma he reckoned you would grow up to be like her—a gentle, pliant wife. He never knew the real you."

"Oh, Aunt! Can that be true? I really thought I loved him but now I have to admit I can hardly recall his face." Belinda felt ashamed of this admission.

Aunt Henshaw patted her hand. "You've come to your senses, my love. George was a pattern card of elegance and I dare say you would have rubbed along comfortably but a girl with your ardent nature needs a man who will see the fire beneath your calm surface."

"That's all very well, Aunt Letty, but no-one of that sort will want to marry a penniless orphan."

"Fudge! You're not to think like that, in fact don't think about marriage at all. Go and fit yourself out with some new clothes, pretty ones in colours that suit you. No more black. Come out of mourning and enjoy yourself. Write to your godmother in York and propose yourself for a visit. Go about and see more of the world. Keep busy and love will creep up when you least expect it."

Belinda, steeped in novels, did not find this difficult to believe. She was delighted with her aunt's prescription. Having new clothes made was just the tonic she needed.

She and Aunt Henshaw bought yards of muslins and gauzes, crepes and silks, satins and poplins. They pored over the latest fashion books and instructed Miss Miggins, the local seamstress, to make up carriage dresses, walking dresses, evening dresses, pelisses and spencer jackets. In the excitement of the fittings, buying bonnets to match the new outfits, and accessories to go with them, Belinda lost her pallor and put back the flesh she had lost while she had mourned.

When Lady Anselm's cordial reply to her letter came, inviting her dearest godchild to come and stay for as long as she wished, Aunt Henshaw helped her pack her new clothes and ordered a post chaise.

"But Aunt, I can very well go on the stage," Belinda protested.

"You'll do nothing of the kind. You'll travel in comfort as befits a lady. Nothing would be more calculated to give any gentleman of address a disgust of you than to hear you were so pinch-penny as to travel by public stagecoach."

At last all was ready and on a blustery March day, smartly dressed, with rosy cheeks and eyes asparkle, Belinda set off for York.

* * *

Araminta Anselm lived in a very different style from her old friend Letitia Henshaw. They were both childless, both plump widows in their fifties but there the resemblance ended. Lady Anselm's large, airy town house was in the best part of York, it was handsomely furnished and efficiently run by a large staff of servants. Lord Anselm had been rich so his widow wanted for nothing. Unlike Letty, she attired herself in the very latest London fashions.

Belinda was her favourite godchild and she welcomed her with little cries of delight, exclaiming how pretty she had become.

"I declare, you are better looking than either your mamma or Letty was at your age, quite a beauty. So lucky that you have such lovely dark hair; much more fashionable than blonde—and those big grey eyes! We must see if we cannot find you a beau."

Belinda blushed and said she was not hanging out for a husband.

"Nonsense," said her godmother. "A good husband with a prosperous estate is just what you need to provide for you and make you comfortable."

Belinda murmured something about love.

"Fiddlesticks," said Lady Anselm, "I collect Letty's been talking, or you have been reading novels! If she and your mamma had not been so starry-eyed about love, they could have been as rich as I am.

"Look where love got your mamma—no farther than a Yorkshire parsonage. Your father was charming and well-connected but as I told her at the time, third sons of barons seldom have much money, and churchmen are invariably poor. Was I not right?

"As for Letty, she took one look at Edward Henshaw and made up her mind to have him. A country lawyer, I pointed out, is always respectable and genteel but seldom rich."

"My mamma and my aunt were both very happy," Belinda

said in their defence.

Lady Anselm swept this aside. "So was I: and I must tell you, dear child, happiness is much enhanced by wealth."

Belinda then told Lady Anselm she had decided to become a governess and had come to solicit her help. Lady Anselm put up her lorgnettes and stared at Belinda.

"A governess," she said in horrified tones. "Out of the question! My own godchild—a niece of Lord Farlow—to take up a position little better than an upper servant? I thank you, no, Belinda. That will not do."

Belinda was taken aback at this opposition to what she considered an eminently sensible scheme.

"But Godmother, what else can I do?"

"I had thought to take you to London for the season but perhaps not this year, not so soon after your fiancé's death although Letty writes you have been very sensible about your loss." She patted Belinda's hand approvingly.

"That is a generous offer and I am indeed grateful but I do not wish to impose on you or Aunt Letty. And I am not sure that I should like London life: country pursuits are so pleasant."

"Tush, child, exactly like your poor mamma. She threw away her chances with just such sentiments."

Belinda ignored this. "Anyway, dear Lady Anselm, I am sure Papa would wish me to make a push to help myself."

"I hope you have not been reading that outrageous book about women's rights by that odious Wollstonecraft woman," said Lady Anselm severely. "It is trash and should never have been published."

Belinda lowered her eyes and said nothing. She had seen the book in the lending library and had glanced at it but found it boring; books in which dewy-eyed heroines were swept off their feet by masterful men were more to her taste.

Lady Anselm thought for a while, tapping her lorgnettes against her teeth, then appeared to reconsider her judgement.

"Perhaps a spell away from Yorkshire would do you good,

and to be usefully employed would take your mind off your losses. We can always take up a season next year. If you are determined upon this folly, I shall see what can be done. Mind, Belinda, I shall only permit you to go to a thoroughly suitable family.

"I occupy a great deal of my time writing letters, keeping up with the friends of my salad days, thus I have quite a network of gossip and intelligence. I shall throw out some hints. Meanwhile we must socialise—in a quiet way, of course. I am glad to see Letty persuaded you out of black. Mourning puts such a damper on enjoyment."

Araminta Anselm was as good as her word. Letters went out to all points of the compass with her latest news and mentioned casually that an excellent governess, well-bred and well-connected was available. After that, she set out to entertain her godchild. She gave several little soirees and dinner parties and took Belinda to concerts and to the theatre and introduced her to York's society at select balls in private houses. Belinda did not want for partners, but no particular gentleman took her fancy and romance did not seem to be in the air.

As Lady Anselm loved shopping and could afford to buy anything that took her fancy, they often visited the warehouses and shops. Belinda found some of the shops extremely quaint, for parts of York had changed little since the middle ages.

Lady Anselm took pleasure in buying Belinda pretty trinkets and trifles. She had only to admire something for her godmother to purchase it and present it to her. In no time she acquired a charming fan, a pretty Spanish comb to wear in her hair and beautiful Norwich shawl, the price of which made her eyes pop. Belinda tried to demur.

Lady Anselm brushed this aside. "Nonsense, child, it's very becoming. It wants but a few weeks to your birthday so if it makes you uncomfortable to have so expensive an article, consider it a birthday gift in advance. You cannot take exception to a present from your godmother on that occasion and you may be glad of it when you are a governess: I should not wish a protégée of mine to appear at a disadvantage in any company. Those who have taste always recognise the best and think the more of those who wear it."

Belinda expressed her thanks but took care not to admire anything else too freely in case Lady Anselm was moved to buy it for her.

Belinda enjoyed her stay in York and did not neglect Aunt Henshaw but wrote regularly to regale her with accounts of their activities. After six weeks when she was beginning to wonder if she were outstaying her welcome, a morning came when Lady Anselm called her into the drawing room.

Pale spring sunshine streamed in through tall windows lighting up the delicate colours of the washed Chinese carpet and gleamed on the well-polished furniture. Lady Anselm sat in a gilt chair in the sunshine reading through her lorgnettes a letter which she held at arm's length.

"Come and listen to this, Belinda, we may have found the very thing for you. This is from my dear friend Elanita, the Countess of Barton, who lives in Suffolk. She and I were presented at Court together. Your mother and Letty could have been there too had they not declined to do a London season having already settled for your papa and your uncle. Thank goodness my mamma had more ambition than your grandmother, for it was in London that I met Lord Anselm and where Elanita and I became bosom-bows. But I am rambling on to no purpose. You must be longing to know what my letter says.

"Elanita writes that she knows of a family who are in need of a governess for two girls. She thinks it would be admirable for you. She says they live in a charming house near the coast and move in the first circles in the county. Matthew Sheldon, who made a fortune with the East India Company is, like your papa, the younger son of a good family. He's a Nabob, my dear, rich beyond the dreams of avarice, as the saying goes. His wife Viola is the daughter of an Indian Army officer but Sheldon was so in love that he married her despite the difference in their social standing."

"Does that matter?" Belinda asked ingenuously. "Papa never gave a rush for such things."

"Belinda! That attitude may have been very well for a clergyman," said Lady Anselm repressively, looking over her lorgnettes, "but you must never forget your social standing and must never yield up anything due to your consequence. You are on a par with the Sheldons even if you are to be in their employ."

Belinda tried not to smile. "No, Godmother," she said dutifully, "but I haven't secured the post yet."

"We shall ensure that!" said Lady Anselm majestically.

She took Belinda into her boudoir and sat her down at the escritoire and dictated a letter of application detailing Belinda's qualifications. She instructed Belinda to ask for sixty guineas a year.

"Godmother, that seems a tremendous sum!"

"Try for a little more worldliness," Lady Anselm said firmly. "People value you at the worth you put on yourself. It would be folly to ask for less."

She wrote Belinda a glowing reference to enclose with the letter. It was sealed and duly sent off. Within a week, a reply came engaging Belinda and agreeing to her terms. She was to join the family in Suffolk during the second week in May.

Araminta Anselm embraced Belinda and congratulated her.

"You just have time to return to Harrogate. Pack your boxes and take yourself off to Suffolk. I shall miss you, child; it has made me feel young again having you here with me. Don't forget, we are to do a London season next year. Be sure to write to tell me how you go on with the Sheldons."

"Dearest Godmother, how can I thank you? Of course I will write."

Belinda posted back to Harrogate to attend to her boxes and trunks. This time she packed not only her clothes but the books, music, paints, and other things she needed for her new profession. Her birthday passed almost unnoticed in a flurry of packing.

At last she was ready and bade farewell to Aunt Henshaw whom she left with fond regret. Aunt Letty had tears in her eyes as she pressed a new novel into Belinda's hands as a parting gift.

This time Belinda insisted on taking the stage, feeling it was more in keeping with her new status than travelling post. She was keyed up and excited, yet a little apprehensive. This would be her first venture outside her native Yorkshire in all her nineteen years

Chapter Two

The stage coach journey to Suffolk took four days. Belinda disliked it intensely. She'd had no idea how uncomfortable it would be when she'd gaily said to Aunt Henshaw that it was the way for a governess to travel. There were several awkward changes that either kept her hanging about in the cold, or rushing from one coach to the next with scarcely enough time to see her boxes were safely stowed. There were halts that were only long enough for her to gulp a few mouthfuls of scalding coffee before she was recalled to her place. There were stop-overs in uncomfortable inns and, least bearable of all, the companionship on the coaches of disagreeable people.

Belinda felt cold, cramped and thoroughly dishevelled when she stepped down from the stage coach at Ipswich. Her light brown travelling pelisse was creased, her matching bonnet, trimmed with a coquelicot feather, was a little awry and her neat half-boots were dusty. Yet in spite of this, several gentlemen turned to look at her with admiring glances for there was an air about her that spoke of breeding and distinction, and her pretty young face framed in dark curls had the charm of innocence. Belinda hardly noticed the looks of approval; she felt out of charity with the world and was beginning to regret leaving Harrogate and the comfort of Aunt Henshaw's presence.

Suddenly, her fortune changed. A charming young man came forward and greeted her.

"Have I the honour of addressing Miss Farrington?" he enquired raising his tall hat.

Belinda looked up at him admiring his fair good looks. "I am she," she said with a smile, immediately feeling better.

"Mark Sheldon," he said with a bow. "My mother sent me

to meet you and bring you to Park Place. Are these your boxes?"

On receiving her acknowledgement, he instructed a liveried footman to deal with her luggage. While it was being stowed, Mr Mark Sheldon handed her into a comfortable barouche.

Belinda sank back against the dove-grey upholstery and settled down thankfully to enjoy a more peaceful mode of travel after the horrors of the stage.

As the barouche began to move, Belinda glanced covertly at her companion. Mark Sheldon was fair with a young, fresh face and smiling blue eyes. His manner towards her was charming with none of the condescension her aunt and her godmother had warned must be the lot of a governess. He began to make conversation to put her at her ease.

"Do you know Suffolk, Miss Farrington?"

The carriage bowled smoothly along the post road now they were out of the town. She looked out of the carriage window at the flat, green countryside bathed in Spring sunshine; it was attractive but very different from the rugged Yorkshire moors that she was used to.

"It is my first visit, sir. It seems tranquil and charming."

"Wait until the wind blows," Mark warned her with a smile. "The country is harsh then. Winters here are bleak."

"So they are in Yorkshire, sir. We are often snowed in. We were this year."

"Then you will be prepared: it happens here, too."

It was at that moment when Belinda was beginning to feel comfortable and soothed that there was a check to their smooth pace. She heard a shout and the barouche pulled up abruptly. All the way from Yorkshire Belinda, remembering the perils of journeys undertaken by fictional heroines, had been expecting trouble. Was some disaster about to happen?

"Sir, pray why are we stopping? Is it highwaymen?" She clutched Mark Sheldon's arm apprehensively,

"I doubt it." Mark lowered the window and stuck his head out. When he drew it in again, Belinda saw his eyes were alight with laughter.

"Not a highwayman, Miss Farrington, a riding officer which is almost as bad."

This meant nothing to her. "A riding officer? I don't understand."

"An official appointed by the Board of Customs; doubtless he is looking for smuggled goods." Mark smiled at her. "Don't worry, we've nothing to hide."

Belinda smiled back shyly. She was reassured but sorry that she had made a silly mistake: Papa had warned her time and again that she must not jump to fantastic conclusions, that life was seldom like the world of novels. She hoped Mr. Mark would not think her foolish.

The door of the barouche was opened by a sallow young man in a light blue uniform and black tricorne. Unlike Mark whose hair was cut modishly short with the curls brushed forward, his sandy hair was long and tied back in an old-fashioned queue fastened with a black ribbon. His thin lips pressed tightly together gave him a grim look.

"Cutting up the peace of innocent citizens, again Yardley?" Mark asked in a supercilious drawl. He was not smiling now.

"I wish to search this conveyance, Mr Sheldon. I have reason to believe run goods are hidden in it."

It was apparent to Belinda from the tone of their exchange that they knew each other well and that there was little love lost between them.

Mark Sheldon frowned. "Would you indeed? Well you may not! Miss Farrington, permit me to introduce Lieutenant Frank Yardley: Mr Yardley, this is Miss Belinda Farrington who is come to be governess to my sisters. I collect you don't suspect her of carrying contraband in her portmanteau?"

Yardley glared at Mark then saluted Belinda. "Your servant, Miss Farrington. I regret disturbing you but I must ask you to stand up so that I may look under the seat."

Belinda, brought up to be obedient to authority, was about to comply but Mark's hand checked her. "Indeed she will not:

you exceed your authority, Yardley."

"I insist, sir, and I have dragoons here to back me."

As they glared at each other, Belinda felt the tension rise.

"Very well," Mark said angrily, "note that we submit under protest."

Belinda and Mark stood up; Yardley leant into the carriage, removed the seat cushions and lifted the hinged board below. The cavity revealed was quite empty.

"Now sir, an apology if you please." Mark's voice was hard.

Two spots of colour showed on Yardley's sallow cheeks. He ignored Mark and said to Belinda, "Be good enough to raise the hem of your dress, if you please, Miss Farrington."

Belinda gasped.

Mark was outraged. "She will do nothing of the kind! You cannot believe that Miss Farrington is involved in smuggling. I will not permit such an impropriety with a lady under my protection. This is unpardonable, sir, you'll hear more of it! Foster," Mark called to the coachman, "drive on!"

Yardley stepped back. His face was red—although whether it was with anger or embarrassment, Belinda could not decide. As the vehicle began to move Yardley called after it.

"One day I'll catch you red-handed, Sheldon."

As they once more bowled along through the Suffolk countryside, Belinda sat silent, shaken by this strange encounter. Mark Sheldon continued to fume. At last he spoke.

"My apologies Miss Farrington, you'll think Suffolk is a nest of smugglers."

"Are there really smugglers here?" Shocking though the idea was, Belinda felt a tremor of excitement. She had read of smugglers but had supposed them invented by authors to enliven their narratives.

"Oh yes," Mark said carelessly, "a deal of 'free trade' is carried on hereabouts."

So it was true: Belinda was intrigued.

"Where do smuggled goods come from? Surely not from

France while we are at war?"

Mark shrugged. "The war makes little difference. Brandy, gin, lace, silk and tea still come over on dark nights."

"But that is treating with the enemy. Is it not a treasonable offence?"

"It suits both sides. Englishmen dislike paying excise duty and Frenchmen like our golden guineas."

"But why did Mr Yardley suspect you? How could you be a smuggler? You are a gentleman, not a ruffian."

"Yardley suspects everyone who lives near the coast. As well as the fisher-folk and countrymen who take part, there has to be a Master-smuggler with money and brains to finance and organise the run. Yardley knows it must be some local gentleman."

Belinda shuddered delicately. "Do you know him? He must be a very wicked man."

Mark laughed. "The Master-smuggler is an enigma, no-one knows who he is. But he is not considered wicked here, for everyone is involved. Humble folk earn extra money helping the smugglers, gentlemen are happy to drink the spirits and ladies want their silk and lace at the cheapest price. No-one with half a grain of sense buys goods over the counter at three times the price the free traders charge. Everybody gains except the excisemen. I almost feel sorry for Yardley—he gets no help from anyone."

"Why did he ask me to lift my skirt?" Belinda blushed, she hardly liked to mention this indelicate matter but her curiosity got the better of her.

"That was outrageous but there was a reason. When houses are searched, the local women throw their skirts over contraband. Impertinent fellow: he should never have asked such a thing of a lady."

"I was startled, but no harm was done, thanks to you, sir."

Belinda was flattered by the chivalrous way Mark had defended her. If the rest of his family were like him, being a governess might not prove a hardship after all.

Almost as if he could read her thoughts, Mark said, "Is this your first post? You are nothing like the old tabbies who have taken charge of my sisters up to now."

"I am recently orphaned, sir." Belinda began to explain her circumstances, Papa's death then Mamma's. She fumbled in her reticule for a handkerchief; thinking about dear Papa and sweet gentle Mamma made her feel melancholy. She didn't mention George for whom she no longer felt more than the sad remembrance one feels for any lost friend.

Mark looked at her anxiously. "Pray don't talk about your losses if it upsets you."

"Thank you, sir, but I must get used to doing so." Belinda put her shoulders back and gave him a small smile. "There was not much money from my father's estate so I decided to take up teaching."

Had Aunt Henshaw been there, she would have muttered 'tragedy queen!' and sent Belinda to the right-about. But Mark was sympathetic.

"Poor Miss Farrington. How sad. Have you no brothers or sisters?"

Belinda shook her head, feeling quite sorry for herself.

Mark began to talk cheerfully. "I, on the other hand, have too many! When I have told you about them, you may ask me to turn the coach round and put you on the stage for the north."

Having no brothers, Belinda was quite unused to teasing. She looked up startled but saw there was a twinkle in Mark's eye. He continued.

"There are six of us, four boys and two girls. Clive is the eldest, a top-lofty fellow of five-and-twenty; Will and Simon, known as the harum-scarum boys, are away at school at present, they are sixteen and thirteen. Your charges are pretty Kitty and naughty Sarah—they're fifteen and twelve. Frankly, Miss Farrington, my sisters are hoydens, much in need of a firm hand to turn them into proper young ladies."

Belinda was surprised by this; there had been no details

about her charges in Mrs. Sheldon's letter and she was dismayed to find they were older than she had imagined. She had certainly not expected them to have four brothers, two of whom were older than their governess. She was not sure how she would cope with hoydens for she had no experience of naughtiness: as a child she had been biddable.

Mark grinned at her startled expression. "So shall I ask Foster to turn the coach round?"

"Don't be absurd, sir." Belinda spoke with more confidence than she felt. "You have told me nothing to upset me. I am sure that there is nothing wrong with your sisters that a little reason and good management cannot cure."

She took Mark's smile as a sign of encouragement but later when she had met his sisters, she thought it had probably been amusement at her ill-placed optimism.

Soon after this, the carriage turned off the post road and they drove along narrow lanes for a while until they swept through a pair of handsome gates and along a well-kept drive leading up to Park Place.

It was a large white house in the newly fashionable Gothic style with pointed church-like windows, and balconies in delicately fretted ironwork. It was so light and white, so prettily ornamented, that it reminded Belinda of a wedding cake. The spring sunshine dazzled on the white front and glinted on the glass panes of a large conservatory at the side.

The front door was opened by a stately butler. Mark helped Belinda down while a second footman with powdered hair and crimson velvet livery assisted the footman who had been riding tiger with her boxes. Mark took her in to meet his mother.

"She's bound to be in the conservatory," he said, his eyes twinkling. "I think she prefers her camellias to her children!"

Viola Sheldon was a small, plump woman with a soft, pretty face framed in golden hair streaked with white. She gave Belinda a cordial welcome and ordered Silver, the butler, to bring in tea.

As Belinda drank her tea, Mrs. Sheldon scrutinised her. "Your letter stated you were nineteen. I must say, you look even younger."

Belinda blushed and fibbed a little, not wanting to admit it was only one week since her nineteenth birthday. "Indeed, ma'am, I am nearly twenty."

Mrs. Sheldon sighed. The girl was far younger and much better looking than any governess she had employed before, but she had certain qualities that overrode this objection. Besides her many accomplishments and her fluent French, Belinda was of impeccable lineage and had that indefinable air of breeding that Mrs. Sheldon wanted for her girls. She was not worried that Belinda's beauty would prove a snare for her elder sons: part of the girl's charm was her naivety. Clive was sophisticated and would find her too simple while Mark, who might have been smitten, was off to India in the autumn.

"I cannot tell you how glad I am to have you here, Miss Farrington," Mrs. Sheldon said, "I had begun to despair of ever finding the right sort of governess for my girls. When Lady Barton told me that the god-daughter of her bosom-bow, Lady Anselm, was looking for a situation and that you were also the niece of Lord Farlow, it seemed like the answer to prayer."

Belinda smiled. She had been brought up by her Papa not to pay much attention to social consequence but she could see it was of great importance to Viola Sheldon. She recollected what her godmother had told her about Mr. and Mrs. Sheldon's inequality of rank.

"I want you to teach my girls to be lady-like," said Mrs. Sheldon firmly. "I should like them to be well-informed but not too knowing for men seldom take to clever women. It is more important for them to be pretty-behaved. At present they are rather wild. Their last governess was a sad mistake, elderly and ineffectual—but with your breeding and accomplishments, I shall expect something very different from you! You may be as strict as you like: I shall not interfere as long as you get results."

Belinda was glad to have her task set out clearly although she wasn't sure she knew how to be strict.

Next, Belinda met Mr. Sheldon, a neatly dressed, red-faced man. His stoutness and his bald head might have made him a figure of fun, but she could see he was not a man to trifle with: he had the air of one used to command. He looked her up and down with evident approval.

"New governess, hey?"

Belinda inclined her head and curtsied.

"M'son tells me you were insulted by the riding officer. Apologies, Miss Farrington, he shall smart for it! Man's a fool to suspect anyone at Park Place of smuggling." He rubbed his hands together. "Hope you'll be happy here and that you'll knock some sense into those giddy girls' heads."

As Mrs. Sheldon took her upstairs to the schoolroom to meet the 'giddy girls', she gave Belinda further instructions.

"You will dine with the family, if you please Miss Farrington. I wouldn't want a niece of Lord Farlow to have suppers on a tray in the schoolroom as our other governesses did. But I shall expect you to be on duty at all times, making those girls behave as they ought.

"My husband and sons breakfast early, I have a tray in my room and you and the girls will be served in the schoolroom. Nuncheon is taken at noon. We keep country hours here and dine at half past five o'clock."

The schoolroom suite was on the topmost floor. Besides the schoolroom itself, there were two bedrooms. Belinda's was next to that of her charges.

As Mrs. Sheldon threw open the schoolroom door two girls got up from the table, dropped wobbly curtsies and looked Belinda over with guarded expressions. Belinda smiled in what she hoped was a friendly and encouraging manner.

Kitty, the older of the two, had creamy skin and curly, light brown hair—Mark was right, she was pretty. Sarah was sturdy and resembled her father. Her tip-tilted nose was sprinkled with freckles and her eyes held a glint of mischief.

"This is Miss Farrington, your new governess; you are to do everything she tells you."

The younger girl blurted out indignantly, "Do what she tells us? That's not fair, Mamma, she's hardly older than Kitty and certainly not as old as Mark or Clive."

Belinda felt a blush creeping up over her cheeks. She did not know how to answer this but Mrs. Sheldon saved her the trouble. Her eyebrows drew together in anger and she slapped Sarah's face.

"Behave yourself! Don't dare to argue with me, Miss, or I shall speak to Papa."

As she turned and left the room, she gave Belinda a tight little smile. It seemed that Mrs. Sheldon couldn't wait to wash her hands of the management of her daughters. Belinda was to discover that Viola Sheldon was not a doting mother; as Mark had said. She was more interested in the exotic blooms in her conservatory than in her daughters. She wanted them changed into well-conducted adults with as little trouble to her as possible. What Belinda, green and gullible, could not guess was what a difficult task that was going to be.

Next morning, as Belinda, Kitty and Sarah sat at the table in the schoolroom eating bread and butter and drinking chocolate, Belinda regarded the girls' table manners with dismay.

"Sit up straight, if you please," she said briskly. "Don't put your elbows on the table. I hope I shan't have to recommend to your mamma that we use backboards. I'm sure we can achieve refined deportment with a little attention and effort."

Belinda smiled but the girls looked resentful. However, they sat straighter and began to behave better. Optimistically, Belinda felt sure she could manage them.

After breakfast, she decided to test their penmanship, she gave them a time-table to copy. With a flourish, Kitty wrote at the top of hers, Catherine Sheldon, May 1812.

"Very neat, Kitty, carry on."

Sarah's heading was so scrawled and spattered that it was unreadable.

Belinda said kindly, "Your trouble, Sarah, is that your pen is incorrectly made." Watched by two pairs of hostile hazel eyes, she proceeded to demonstrate how a quill should be prepared.

It was not until later that day that Belinda met their eldest brother. He had been away on a visit and returned home just as she and the girls were going down to the garden for a brisk walk to give them an appetite for nuncheon.

Kitty who was beside the landing window cried, "Look, Miss Farrington, here is our brother Clive. Doesn't he look splendid? Slap up to the echo, as usual."

Although Belinda had no brothers, she could recognise a cant expression. She was sure this was the kind of thing Mrs. Sheldon expected her to frown upon.

"Kitty! What a shocking piece of slang. You should say 'elegant'."

She glanced out of the window which overlooked the stable yard. Descending from a curricle was a fashionably dressed young man. Clive Sheldon was tall, his long legs were encased in well-polished top-boots, his broad shoulders were set off by a six-caped driving coat of drab embellished with pearl buttons like small saucers. A low-crowned beaver hat sat on short brown curls. The impression of a man of fashion was completed by a large nosegay in his button hole.

Belinda saw what Kitty meant by 'slap up to the echo' but there was such an air of self-confident arrogance about him that she had a feeling she was not going to like Mr. Clive Sheldon.

By the time the schoolroom party reached the hall, Clive was there too. Kitty and Sarah greeted him eagerly but with a touch of restraint indicating their awe of this god-like person. They introduced Belinda but although he had a warm smile for his sisters, his greeting to her was cool and formal. He had a powerful presence which, in spite of her first impression, made Belinda's heart flutter but, she reflected with a moment's regret, he would hardly condescend to notice a mere governess. She did not suppose that they would see very much of one another: she could not have guessed that she and Clive were to become closer acquainted and to cross swords that very afternoon.

The trouble began after nuncheon. Belinda sent the girls to lie down upon their beds and rest while she retired to the schoolroom to write to Aunt Henshaw and Lady Anselm to apprise them of her safe arrival. She was engrossed in composing her letters when Kitty came in with a self-important air.

"If you please, Miss Farrington," she said in a smug voice, "Sarah is locked in the linen room."

"Good grief, how came this about?"

"I thought she had gone to the necessary house but she was away so long, I went to find her."

"But why is she locked in? Was it by accident?"

"Oh no." Kitty was enjoying herself. "She did it on purpose."

Belinda's heart sank. She had expected the girls to test her authority, but not so soon.

"Come," she said with coolness she didn't feel, "take me to the linen room."

Kitty led her down to the floor below, pointed out the door, stood back and watched with interest.

Belinda knocked. "Sarah! Come out this instant!"

There was no reply, but Belinda heard soft scuffling. She spoke severely.

"This is very naughty, Sarah: by rights, you should be punished but if you come out at once, we'll say no more about it."

There was a giggle from the other side of the door. "Make me!" said Sarah.

Belinda had a sinking feeling of despair. Was she to be

proved incompetent so soon? She tried cunning.

"I suppose the key is too stiff for such a little girl to turn. If you put it under the door I will let you out."

"But I don't want to come out," said Sarah with a maddening giggle.

Belinda drew Kitty aside and asked, "Is there a window to the linen room?"

Kitty nodded.

"Show me where it is."

Belinda took her by the hand and they went out to the stable yard.

"Bring a ladder and follow me," Belinda said to a gardener's boy who was lurking there talking to a stable lad. "Now, Kitty, point out the linen room window."

Kitty's eyes were sparkling with enjoyment but seeing Belinda's grim expression, she tried to look serious. "This one."

When the ladder was placed against the window, Belinda instructed the boy to hold it firmly. She lifted her skirt and put her foot on the lowest rung.

Kitty gasped. "Miss Farrington! Surely you are not going up?"

"I most certainly am. Wait here."

"I should not if I were you, Miss Farrington. Indeed, ma'am, I would not." Kitty's voice held a note of alarm.

Belinda would have liked to be dissuaded but she saw it as her duty to get Sarah out. Sick with apprehension, she began to climb, not daring to look down. Slowly, step by step, she rose to what seemed a dangerous height. As she drew level with the window, she put her face against the glass and peered in. What she saw made her almost fall off the ladder. She was not at the linen room window but outside Clive Sheldon's bedroom! Staring at her was Mr. Clive in his shirt sleeves, frozen in the act of tying his cravat. Beside him stood Jevons, his manservant, round-eyed and open-mouthed.

Clive strode to the window and threw up the lower half.

"Miss Farrington! What, pray, is the meaning of this?"

Belinda felt herself to be in danger of slipping. She held the top rung tightly and wished herself a thousand miles away.

"I-it is not what you think, sir," she stammered, deeply embarrassed, "I am trying to rescue your sister Sarah."

His eyebrows rose in surprise and disdain. "Sarah is not here, I am not in the habit of holding my sisters captive."

"N-no indeed sir, she has locked herself in the linen room. I intended to remonstrate with her through the window but seem to have approached the wrong room."

"I see. Well, you had better come in rather than attempt the perilous descent." Clive's frown had gone and his lips were twitching. Belinda realised indignantly that he was laughing at her, but he seemed perfectly serious as he helped her into his room. She was pink with mortification.

"Jevons, stop gaping like a booby and offer Miss Farrington some hartshorn to revive her."

"That won't be necessary, thank you. As soon as I have caught my breath, I'll have the ladder moved and try again."

"I will deal with Sarah," said Clive in an icy tone.

Miserably, Belinda followed him downstairs and out into the garden.

"You here too, Kitty?" he said severely. "I collect it was you who gave Miss Farrington the false information?"

Belinda, who had charitably assumed that it was a mistake, looked at Kitty sharply and saw that Clive was right.

"I told her not to go up," Kitty said virtuously.

"While hoping that she would!" said her brother scornfully.

It was the work of a moment for Clive to move the ladder and climb it. A sharp word brought Sarah to the window where she meekly handed over the key. Clive gave it to Belinda and strode away without another word.

Once the door was unlocked, Belinda had no trouble making Sarah come out. She swept the girls off to the schoolroom where she delivered herself of a scalding lecture which relieved her feelings and seemed to impress Kitty and

Sarah. They hung their heads and apologised. Belinda sat them down and told them to write in their best handwriting one hundred times, I must at all times behave with decorum.

Not long after they had bent their heads to the task, there was a tap on the door. It was Clive wanting a word in private with Belinda. Bidding the girls go on writing, she stepped out into the corridor, closing the door behind her.

"I have yet to thank you, sir, for helping me out of my foolish predicament," Belinda began, smiling at him.

There was no answering smile from Mr. Clive Sheldon. He spoke in measured tones. "Miss Farrington, my sisters have been indulged too often and have run wild too long. If their governess makes herself ridiculous by climbing ladders, they will hardly profit by her example and mend their ways. I don't know which was more idiotic—allowing Sarah to go off by herself, or trying to climb a ladder instead of sending for a servant to do it."

Belinda's smile froze, she drew a deep breath. "Perhaps I did not set a good example nor pursue a prudent course but I must tell you, sir, that I have your mother's permission to deal with the girls as I think fit. My unfamiliarity with the house caused me to intrude upon you and for that I apologise. Rest assured, sir, I shall take good care that the girls and I do not inconvenience you further."

Her cheeks flaming, Belinda turned on her heel and re-entered the schoolroom leaving Clive without opportunity to reply. She was shaking with anger. How odious he was! How unfortunate that he, not sympathetic Mark, had rescued her. She sat down in the schoolroom to let her cheeks and her temper cool.

The girls must have heard the raised voices for she detected sympathy in their eyes. For the rest of the day, they behaved like angels. Nevertheless, she decided they must be punished and decreed they should not go down to dinner with the family but should dine in the schoolroom so she was obliged to explain the incident to Mrs. Sheldon.

"What an afternoon you've had, Miss Farrington," she said languidly when Belinda had told her tale. "Experience has inured me to surprise at my children's mischief. Let us hope that before long your influence will stop these high-spirited pranks. I will instruct Silver to serve a very plain dinner in the schoolroom."

Belinda's spirits were further lowered when just before dinner, she learned that the escapade was the talk of the household. Mark stopped her on the stairs, his blue eyes brimming with laughter.

"So Sarah has been playing the monkey again and the wretched Kitty has landed you in trouble with Clive! I hear you had one of his freezing set-downs. He's a hypocrite, you know."

"How so?"

"He was a rip himself once upon a time. I'll have you know he once put a toad inside his tutor's night cap and thought it a capital tease."

Belinda was amazed. "Surely not, not Mr. Clive?"

"Indeed he did and earned one of Papa's fiercest tongue-lashings. Clive's really a great gun although he may seem a trifle starched up until you get to know him."

That evening as Belinda lay in bed she reviewed her first two days at Park Place. She had failed miserably in her first confrontation with her charges and made herself foolish in Clive's eyes. As for his unfair scolding, she knew she shouldn't care for his good opinion but such was the impression he had made upon her that she found that she did.

As she settled down for the night, she promised herself that the coming day would be very different. However it was a rash promise that Fate had no intention of allowing her to fulfil.

Chapter Three

Belinda's bedroom overlooked the stable yard and during the night, she was woken by the sound of muffled hooves on the cobbles. She lay in bed wondering what could be going on there. Even her fertile imagination primed by her novel reading could not suggest an answer. Consumed by curiosity, she slipped out of bed and went to the window but it was pitch dark and she could see nothing. She stood a while listening, but the noises had ceased. She yawned and, deciding her imagination must have been playing tricks, she returned to bed and was soon asleep again.

At breakfast next morning in the schoolroom she asked the girls if they had been disturbed in the night by strange noises.

Instead of answering directly, Kitty countered with another question. "Did you hear something?"

Belinda was cautious. "I could not be sure."

"If you heard noises, depend upon it, it was the Gentlemen—the free traders," said Kitty.

Belinda had almost forgotten about the smuggling Mark had mentioned; the idea still seemed unreal in spite of her meeting with the riding officer.

"Don't be absurd, Kitty. What would smugglers be doing here?"

"Delivering Papa's brandy or Mamma's tea," said Sarah knowingly, "or hiding a cargo in the stables."

"I think that unlikely," Belinda said and was dismayed to see the girls exchanging grins. Quickly, she changed the subject.

"We are going into the grounds to sketch this morning."

"Must we, Miss Farrington?" Sarah said plaintively. "I can't draw at all well."

"All the more reason to practise," said Belinda firmly.

"Drawing is no fun," wailed Kitty. "I wanted to go riding."

"Your mamma wishes you to pursue lady-like accomplishments and painting water-colours is one of them."

"Lady-like fiddle!" said Kitty contemptuously.

Belinda ignored this and sent the girls to put on shady straw hats while she fetched her own bonnet and a light merino shawl in case her round dress of lemon muslin was not warm enough. Armed with sketching books, the schoolroom party set forth.

* * *

The grounds of Park Place had been laid out in the latest fashion by Humphry Repton, the celebrated landscape designer and were kept in a state of excellence by a team of gardeners. After threading their way through a rhododendron shrubbery, they followed a path down to the lake which was surrounded by willow trees, artistically weeping into the water.

"How charming this is," said Belinda with real pleasure. "We will sketch today and put on the colours tomorrow."

The girls listened with ill-concealed resentment as she gave them a lecture on how a picture should be composed, then bent their heads over their books and began to draw. Belinda was congratulating herself on their docility when Sarah espied a diversion and let out a shriek.

"Oh, Miss Farrington, look! A dear little kitten is in that tree. It is stuck fast and cannot get down."

Tossing aside their books and pencils, Kitty and Sarah ran to the tree where a shivering tabby kitten was mewing piteously in the crook of a branch, high above their heads. Although they were genuinely concerned, the girls were extremely glad to have an excuse to stop sketching. Belinda followed her charges, wishing the kitten twenty miles away.

"What shall we do?" asked Kitty as the kitten ignored her

impassioned pleas to come down.

"I dare say if it got itself up, it can get itself down." Belinda said.

Sarah thought this heartless. "Well it can't, then. Poor little thing, we must rescue it." Before Belinda could stop her, she threw off her hat and started to climb the tree with scant regard for her delicate apple green muslin dress.

"Sarah, come down!"

Belinda might as well have talked to the wind for all the notice Sarah took.

"Don't worry about her, Miss Farrington," said Kitty kindly. "Our brother Will taught her to climb—she's quite a hand."

"But she must not." Belinda was agitated. "Your mamma relies upon me to stop her doing such unladylike things. Come down, Sarah."

Sarah took no notice nor did she pause when her dress caught on a branch and tore.

"Can you reach it?" Kitty asked anxiously.

"No, and I am stuck now. Do come up, Kitty and see if you can free me."

Kitty was quite willing but Belinda stopped her. "I will try to release Sarah."

Belinda removed her bonnet and summoning her courage, began to follow her pupil. It was her first attempt at tree climbing and she climbed awkwardly, not having been trained by a brother. Before long, her gown ripped. Laboriously moving from foothold to handhold and not daring to look down, at length, she came within reach of Sarah.

At that moment, the kitten decided it had had enough of the tree and began to descend. It jumped, claws spread, onto Sarah's head.

Sarah shrieked.

The cat leapt from Sarah's head onto Belinda's; its claws became entangled in her topknot, disarranging the cluster of dark curls. Belinda cried out as the kitten scrambled down her back, tearing her muslin further and raking her skin as it slid, claws extended.

The kitten's third leap took it to the ground where it scampered off into the bushes, ignoring Kitty's blandishments. The exasperated rescuers were left clinging to the tree like disconsolate monkeys.

It was at that unfortunate moment that, to Belinda's chagrin, they were discovered by Clive who happened to be passing the lake. He took one look and burst out laughing.

"Trees instead of ladders today, Miss Farrington? I collect climbing is something of a passion with you."

Belinda was mortified. "Oh hush, sir, do not tease. Help me down and I will explain."

Clive gave her his hand and she was able to scramble down. He then lifted Sarah and put her on the ground. He was in a good humour and grinned at his sisters.

"Run back to the house, Sarah, you little imp. Change your dress—you look like a sweep's child! Kitty, go with her and help."

Belinda bristled. She had been about to give these instructions herself. Clive's usurpation of her authority infuriated her. What a self-important busybody he was: she couldn't remember when she had taken anyone in such strong aversion.

"Mr. Clive, this is the second time you have given Sarah an order that should have come from me! If I am to influence your sisters, they must learn to mind my commands. If you please, do not instruct them in my presence."

His expression was no longer amused, to be reprimanded by a chit of a governess affronted him. His eyes hardened and he said coldly, "As this is the second time I have found you setting my sisters a bad example, I feel entirely justified in giving them instructions. I wonder what my mother can be about employing a hen-witted governess so young and irresponsible as to be in need of a governess herself."

"Unhandsome, sir, and unfair! I am nineteen and have had an excellent education..."

"But still have a great deal to learn! I recommend to you the maxim you made my sisters write out yesterday—I must at all times behave with decorum."

"How dare you, sir, you are insufferable!"

"Then you need suffer me no longer. Good day."

He strode off leaving Belinda with tears of anger brimming.

Back at the house while she was washing and changing she regretted speaking out so boldly. True, she had been in the wrong but he had not known the circumstances; it was no excuse for Clive to ring a peal over her. When her mirror showed her how she had appeared to him, dark hair awry, grey eyes angry, dress torn and dirt on face and hands, she was aghast.

Without siblings or school fellows to tease her, Belinda had never acquired the habit of laughing at herself and was inclined to take herself far too seriously. She had been stung by Clive's remark about her youth and unsuitability for her post and on sober reflection, thought perhaps he was right. She was unsuited to dealing with high-spirited romps: perhaps she ought to offer Mrs. Sheldon her resignation. It seemed that becoming a governess had been a sad mistake.

When Belinda was neatly dressed again and in a calmer frame of mind, she set the girls an essay to write, and went in search of Mrs. Sheldon. She found her in the conservatory, tending her flowers. When she told her what had happened, Viola Sheldon brushed Belinda's doubts aside and would not hear of her giving up so easily.

"That silly incident is not sufficient reason to quit your post. I'll be frank with you, Miss Farrington, those girls are such a handful, I despaired of finding a governess who could deal with them. Your application and Lady Anselm's recommendation saved my sanity. To find someone young enough to keep up with them who was well educated and a lady was more than I hoped for."

"But dear ma'am, I am so ashamed. I haven't been here a se'ennight and already I've been in two dreadful scrapes. Mr. Clive doesn't think I am fit to have the care of his sisters..."

Viola Sheldon swung round as if she had been stung. "And what has it to do with him, pray? That's just like him to fly up into the boughs and to meddle with my arrangements. Well, he shall not! He is far too fond of his opinions and so I shall tell him."

Venomously, she nipped off a dead flower as if she wished it were her eldest son's head. "At the outset I gave you permission to deal with those vexatious girls as you saw fit. And I cannot possibly be without a governess just now. We are facing trouble and the sort of shabby-genteel, mimsy governess Clive has in mind would be quite useless."

"Trouble, ma'am?"

"The boys at Westminster have been rusticated for some silly prank so Will and Simon are coming home. How Kitty and Sarah will behave with their brothers' encouragement, I dare not think. There must be a strong hand on the reins to check their conduct. I implore you, Miss Farrington, do not leave me in my hour of need."

"Of course I will not go, ma'am if you do not wish it."

Belinda felt better knowing she was needed but was not entirely confident she would be able to stop the girls falling into mischief, but she was determined to try.

Mrs. Sheldon sighed deeply. "It is a sore trial to have unruly children. You, having not had brothers, have no notion what tricks boys get up to."

This was true, but Belinda was sure Mrs. Sheldon was exaggerating. She soothed her employer and promised she would not mention resigning again.

"Thank you, Miss Farrington. You are not to worry about Clive and his high-flown ideas. As soon as he comes in, I shall give him a piece of my mind."

"Not on my account, ma'am. I do not mind what he says

so long as you don't feel I am unworthy of your trust."

"No, indeed, Miss Farrington. You are to do whatever you think best with the girls." Mrs. Sheldon dismissed her with a vague wave of her hand and turned back to her beloved plants.

As Belinda went off to the schoolroom to see how the essays were progressing, she wondered what the heroine of a three-decker romance would do in her place. Although these intrepid maidens seemed able to deal in sanguine fashion with ghosts, monsters, pirates and mysterious locked rooms, she had never read a book in which an inexperienced governess had to cope with self-willed tomboys and rebellious youths. Out in the real world, she was discovering that life bore little resemblance to fiction.

Next morning when Belinda decreed sketching again, Kitty said, "If we must sketch, Miss Farrington, could we not do so by the sea? Our own grounds are so confining."

"We could collect seashells, too," said Sarah eagerly.

"Why not?" Belinda fell in with their suggestions. If the girls were doing something they enjoyed, they were more likely to be tractable.

A conveyance was ordered from the stable and as they set out, Kitty and Sarah were laughing and joking. It was a warm day and Belinda was able to admire the countryside at its smiling, springtime best. The small fields enclosed by neat hedges were very different from the rolling moors of her native Yorkshire and reminded her of children's toy farms. She was interested to see the hawthorn hedges blooming in Suffolk a full month earlier than they would be in the north.

Near the sea, the land was open heath and dunes of shifting sand held together with clumps of spiky grass, sea lavender and thrift. They got out among the dunes and left the carriage with Ben, the young undergroom who had driven them, and walked onto the shingle beach.

The sea was like a sheet of puckered grey silk, the sun glinting on its wrinkled surface. The tide was out, exposing an expanse of shiny grey mud and sand. A brisk sea breeze tugged at Belinda's bonnet but it was securely fastened under her chin with cherry ribbons to match the trimming of her grey poplin dress.

Kitty and Sarah, chattering excitedly, began to run along the stony band of shingle. Belinda, following more sedately, sympathised with her charges: she was young enough to feel the urge to run and shout in the bright May sunshine, intoxicated by the briny sea air.

"Don't go too fast," she called, "or you'll turn an ankle."

They laughed and waved but ran on. For a moment she feared they were running away, but was reassured when they stopped from time to time to put shells in a basket.

Her attention was distracted from her charges by the sight of a horseman coming towards her over the dunes. He was wearing the sky-blue uniform and black tricorne of a riding officer. Then she recognised him as the impertinent man who had asked her to raise her skirt when last they met. She had taken him in strong dislike but there was no way she was going to be able to avoid an encounter. She composed herself and tried to appear aloof.

He jumped off his horse and strode towards her smiling. "Miss Farrington, how lucky to meet you here—I have been wanting to see you to apologise for my discourtesy the other day."

"There is no need," she said coldly, avoiding his eyes.

"Indeed there is. I was so anxious to make an arrest that I overstepped the bounds of what is acceptable. There is something about Mr. Mark Sheldon that I cannot like."

Belinda began to walk on. "Really? I find him pleasant and courteous." Mark, with his laughing eyes was her favourite Sheldon. His manner was vastly to be preferred to Clive's cold superiority.

It seemed Yardley was thick-skinned and not at all put off by her repressive answers; he walked beside her, his horse's reins looped over his arm. "How are you settling at Park

Place?"

"It is a charming house and the Sheldons are kind."

"When Sheldon said you were his sisters' governess, I didn't believe him. You don't look like a governess. You're so young and pretty I thought you must be a French countess come with the smugglers; Mark Sheldon's accomplice." There was admiration in his eyes.

Belinda was amused by this heavy handed compliment but not to be won over by flattery. "I have only just become a governess, this is my first post."

Yardley was so interested that Belinda thawed a little and went on.

"I am alone in the world and have to earn my living—I am an orphan and my fiancé was killed in the fighting in the Peninsula." Belinda could talk about her losses these days without feeling sorry for herself. As she mentioned George, she realised she had not thought about him for weeks.

Yardley expressed his sympathy but Belinda did not want to go on talking about herself. "How do you come to be in the excise service, Mr. Yardley?"

He was happy to tell her. "My father is a merchant who deals in tea and spices. I grew up hearing him cursing smugglers whose undutied goods were ruining him. My elder brother works with him in the business but there was not room for me so it seemed logical for me to apply to the Board of Customs for a post and work against smugglers."

"Does smuggling do your father's trade so much harm?"

"Indeed it does. Thirteen million pounds of tea are consumed in this country every year. Try to guess how many pounds have duty paid on them."

Belinda shook her head.

"Duty is paid on only five-and-a-half-million pounds! Imagine how many people buy smuggled tea to the ruination of merchants like my father."

Belinda was amazed; no wonder Frank Yardley hated smugglers. "I'm afraid I'm very ignorant, what does a riding officer do?"

"Spends most of his life in the saddle—riding. Smuggling is a way of life on this coast. Fishermen and farm labourers can earn more in a single night's smuggling than in two months' ordinary work. I, with only six men, have to patrol dozens of miles of coast to try to stop them."

"Why did you think you'd find contraband in the Sheldon's barouche?" Belinda asked.

"There had been a run the night before, I thought Mr. Mark was distributing the cargo. I'm convinced that someone at Park Place is the smugglers' leader and financier. The Master-smuggler must be either the old man, Mr. Clive or Mr. Mark."

Belinda was shocked. "How can you say so! Mr. Sheldon is rich so he would have no need to smuggle contraband; Mr. Clive is straight-forward and upright, and Mr. Mark is honest and charming."

"Is that how they seem to you?" Frank Yardley's smile was crooked. "How do you feel about smuggling, Miss Farrington."

She said without hesitation, "I think it is wrong."

"I'm relieved to hear you say so. Would you be willing to help me to entrap the Master-smuggler?"

Belinda gasped; this was almost as much of a shock as his asking her to raise her skirt. "I? How could I possibly be of assistance?"

"You live at Park Place. You could watch the Sheldons and tell me if anything suspicious happens."

Belinda was agitated by this. If she refused, Yardley would think she supported the law breakers: if she agreed to spy, she would be abusing a position of trust. He seemed to see no impropriety in his request but she was outraged by it and spoke angrily.

"That would be most improper. You cannot ask me to do such a thing! Anyway, I do not believe they are involved. Say no more, Mr. Yardley, your idea is monstrous!"

The riding officer's expression hardened. "Think about it, Miss Farrington. I'm determined to break this ring and I'll do it with or without your help but you could make it swifter and easier." He touched his hat, swung into the saddle and rode off.

Belinda stood, staring out to the horizon, her pleasure in the sun and sea spoiled, her thoughts in turmoil. Although she had rejected Yardley's theory she wondered if it could be true. Not Matthew Sheldon, certainly—but what about Clive, could it be him? He had been away the night of the run but that could have been because he organised it. It couldn't be carefree Mark with his laughing eyes and dimpled smile. It was easier to think ill of Clive who had wounded her feelings—and yet it was Clive not Mark who made her heart flutter.

Kitty and Sarah ran up in tearing spirits, laughing and joking, making her start.

"Was that the riding officer you were talking to?" asked Sarah in a tone of disapproval. "What did he want?"

"Flirting, I'll be bound," said Kitty. "He's not a suitable beau for you, Miss Farrington, quite beneath you."

"Don't be nonsensical." Belinda was blushing. "Your brother introduced us the other day and he was making polite conversation."

"Prying to see if you knew anything about smuggling, more like," said Sarah darkly. "Don't talk to him, Miss Farrington or the local people will think you're his spy."

This was too near the truth for Belinda's liking so she changed the subject. She admired their shells and promised to show them how to use them to decorate a box and to make a picture frame. To the girls' delight, she agreed it was too windy for sketching and they walked back to the carriage.

As they drove home, Belinda noticed that in spite of the wind, the sails of a windmill close to the shore were not moving. She remarked upon it and was astonished when the girls burst out laughing, clutching each other as they giggled.

Ben, the groom, was grinning too, although he kept his eyes straight ahead.

"What is so funny? Please share the joke with me."

"Look behind you: the windmill at Redfield is the same," Kitty said.

"But why, and why is it so funny?"

"We shouldn't tease," Kitty said, trying not to laugh. "It's not the windmills that are the joke, it's you, not understanding. Round here the windmills are known as the smugglers' telegraph. Whenever a riding officer is spotted, the nearest miller sets his sails up straight. The signal is repeated at the next mill and within a quarter of an hour, a message can be passed from Yarmouth to Horsey that he is about. They have another way of setting the sails when the Revenue cutters are sighted at sea."

"As we go through the village," added Sarah, "you'll see in the window of the first cottage a white china cat facing the street. That means a riding officer is nearby. If the cat has its back to the street, the coast is clear."

Belinda began to see that the riding officer did indeed have every man's hand against him. He was sorely in need of aid but although she disapproved of smuggling, she was not inclined to help him—nor should he expect it.

He would have to catch the Master-smuggler without her assistance.

Chapter Four

The schoolroom window overlooked the drive. Sarah, who was supposed to be writing an essay on 'Elizabeth I or Mary Queen of Scots: who was the better queen?' heard the sound of carriage wheels on the gravel. Welcoming the distraction, she jumped up, ran to the window and peered out trying to see who had come to call.

Belinda remonstrated. "Sarah, come back here at once! I did not give you permission to leave your work."

Sarah grinned. "Sorry, Miss Farrington."

Kitty looked at her sister expectantly. "Well?"

"To show curiosity is vulgar," Belinda pronounced. "Get on with your essays."

"Who is it?" hissed Kitty.

"Wouldn't you like to know." Sarah was so smug that Belinda could have smacked her. "If you must know, Kitty, it's Mrs. Hallingbury with her precious golden haired Isabella. Come to pay Mamma a morning call, but more likely so Isabella can throw out lures for Clive."

Now Belinda was the one who was curious but after her strict admonitions to her pupils she could hardly ask for enlightenment: however, gratification came soon. Richard, the footman, came up to the schoolroom and announced that the young ladies and their governess were required to join Mrs. Sheldon and her guests in the drawing room.

"Huh," said Kitty scornfully, "they don't want to see us—they have met us a thousand times. Isabella wants to look you over, Miss Farrington, to see whether you will put her nose out of joint. She doesn't usually bother with females but she dotes on Clive and doesn't wish for competition."

"I do hope he doesn't offer for Isabella," Sarah said. "She is the most selfish girl alive and quite nasty."

"Speculation about your brother's affairs is as vulgar as curiosity," Belinda said. "Tidy your hair and please try not to shame me in front of your mamma's visitors."

While the girls hurried off to their room giggling, Belinda went to her own room and checked her appearance in her mirror. Her high necked dress of dark green was rather dull so she added a cameo brooch at her throat and took out her fine Norwich shawl and draped it across her elbows. She was pleased with the effect; the shawl added an air of distinction to her appearance which gave her confidence.

Kitty and Sarah entered the drawing room first and curtsied to their mother's guests. Belinda made a mental note that she still had to attend to those unsteady curtsies.

Introductions were made. Mrs. Hallingbury was a discontented looking woman drably dressed in shades of brown. However, Miss Isabella Hallingbury made up for her mother's dullness: she was wearing an outfit the unsuitability of which almost took Belinda's breath away. Perched on her golden curls was a confection of lace and flowers and her cornflower blue satin dress was cut low at the neck and trimmed with a profusion of swansdown. The ensemble would have caused a stir in Bond Street at the height of the season and for a morning call in the country it was startling in the extreme, but Isabella's complacent expression showed that she was greatly pleased with herself.

Belinda did not think Miss Hallingbury could be more than twenty but already her pink and white complexion was marred by frown lines and her rosebud mouth was set in a pout.

Belinda hoped her smile would be taken as a sign of affability rather than the amusement she felt at such a vulgar spectacle. But the smile was wiped from Belinda's face by Miss Hallingbury's first remark.

"A Norwich shawl! What an extravagant item for a governess!" Isabella looked her over and remarked disdainfully, "At fifty pounds, I dare swear it must have cost you more than a year's salary."

Kitty and Sarah gasped and Mrs. Sheldon frowned.

Belinda replied sweetly, "I've no notion of its cost, Miss Hallingbury; it was a present from my godmother."

Mrs. Sheldon said quickly, "Miss Farrington's godmother is Lady Anselm, whom I'm sure you know, Mrs. Hallingbury, and her uncle is Lord Farlow."

This information did not seem to please Mrs. Hallingbury who looked surprised and peered rudely at Belinda through her lorgnettes. "I know of Lady Anselm of course: her rout parties during the season are famous."

"And are you taking Isabella to London for the season again?" Mrs. Sheldon enquired with just a hint of emphasis on the word 'again'.

Sarah whispered to Belinda, "She's done two seasons without an offer."

Belinda frowned but inwardly she was laughing.

Isabella seemed impervious to Mrs. Sheldon's implied criticism. "We haven't decided yet, there are many amusements to be enjoyed here in Suffolk at this time of year. I was hoping to see Clive for I have a notion to get up a picnic expedition and need his help."

"Oh Lor'," Kitty muttered.

"He is not here at the moment, he is out riding with his father. I am sure he will be delighted to assist you, Isabella. I'll ask him to call on you, shall I?" said Mrs. Sheldon.

"Please do," said Isabella.

Mrs. Hallingbury rose. "Come, Isabella, we have other calls to make. I am glad to see your daughters again, Mrs. Sheldon. They seem in good health and spirits but it is a pity that you have to change governesses so often. It must be disconcerting for them." She looked down her nose at Belinda.

Mrs. Sheldon accompanied her visitors to the door and returned to the drawing room looking aggrieved.

"I beg you will not let my wretched visitors upset you, Miss

Farrington; I could have sunk through the floor when Mrs. Hallingbury was unpleasant and Isabella was rude about your shawl. Her remarks were unpardonable."

"I did not regard it, ma'am," Belinda said without rancour.

"Well I did," said Kitty hotly. "Isabella is quite the most awful girl we know."

"What a pig," said Sarah inelegantly, earning a frown from her mother. "Why shouldn't Miss Farrington have a Norwich shawl? Even were she to come down dripping with diamonds it would be nothing to do with Isabella."

Belinda laughed at this. "I hope, Sarah, that even were I to possess them, I should not be so vulgar as to wear diamonds to receive a morning call." She was surprised and touched at Sarah's support.

"I expect she was jealous because Miss Farrington looked far more elegant than she did," said Kitty. "What a quiz she looked in that dreadful outfit. What can Clive see in her?"

Mrs. Sheldon said, "Now Kitty, we don't know what Clive thinks of her and it is wrong of you to discuss it. I am sorry I asked you to come down, Miss Farrington, but Mrs. Hallingbury most particularly asked to meet the new governess. I wouldn't have had Lord Farlow's niece insulted for the world."

Belinda said, "My aunt and my godmother warned me that governesses are frequently looked down upon so I was not dismayed."

"Looked down upon!" Kitty was indignant. "Not by us. You are worth two of beastly Bella."

At that moment Mark put his head round the door and came in." Did I hear the name of Bella Hallingbury, the girl I love to hate? Don't tell me I've missed her—dear me, how sad." His expression was comical.

Kitty told him of Isabella's hideous outfit and her unwarranted rudeness.

"I'm not surprised—she's a a graceless creature and a designing minx. She is setting her cap at Clive—I hope he's not taken in."

"By whom might I be taken in?" Clive was rubbing his hands together as he joined the company in cheerful mood.

"Beastly Bella. Pray don't have her, Clive!" said Kitty.

Clive's smile disappeared. "When I want your advice, Catherine, I shall inform you. It is the height of vulgarity to speculate about people's private lives."

"That's what Miss Farrington says," Sarah told him virtuously. "She says curiosity and speculation are equally vulgar."

"Good for Miss Farrington." He bestowed a smile on Belinda that warmed her delightfully. "Now, how about some nuncheon, I am starved."

* * *

During the meal of cold fowl, biscuits and fruit Mrs. Sheldon told Clive that Isabella wanted to consult him about a picnic.

"The girl's stark raving mad," said Mark. "It's far too early in the year for such a junket. Ten to one it'll rain on the day she chooses."

"I dare say she's just being kind: I'll call and discuss it with her," Clive promised.

Sarah began to giggle.

"What now, Miss?" Clive asked with mock severity.

"She is bound to want to go in your curricle so she can be alone with you. I don't envy you."

"If that is the case, I shall insist on your squeezing in between us to act as chaperone." He grinned at Sarah, his eyes twinkling.

Belinda warmed to him, thinking how attractive he was when he was in a good humour.

"What about me?" Kitty wanted to know.

"You shall go with Mark and Miss Farrington in the barouche."

"No chance of that. She won't ask Miss Farrington, more's the pity. You should have heard her vulgar remarks about Miss Farrington's shawl," Kitty said.

Clive frowned. "I shall insist that Miss Farrington comes, otherwise I shall decline the invitation."

"Bravo," said Mark. "I was going to refuse but I won't if Miss Farrington's coming." He bowed to her across the table, making Belinda blush. She was much heartened by the Sheldons' kindness and easy acceptance of her contrasting so strongly with the Hallingburys' condescension.

"Of course Miss Farrington must go to look after Kitty and Sarah to see they behave," Mrs. Sheldon said.

"Well we will behave," said Sarah, "but it will be more fun with Miss Farrington."

Belinda felt cheered by this further sign of Sarah's approbation. As they went up to the schoolroom after the meal, she heard Sarah say to Kitty, "What a lark it will be. I shall enjoy playing gooseberry with Clive and Isabella—she'll be so angry."

Belinda smiled. For reasons she would not admit to herself, she was glad that Sarah was to sit between Clive and Isabella on the projected expedition.

* * *

Belinda was beginning to think that Kitty and Sarah would never complete their water colours. A spring shower prevented them from going outdoors the next day, making the girls gleeful, but when Belinda said that instead they could start embroidering samplers, they became sulky. Then, remembering a precept of her papa's—'more flies are caught with honey than vinegar', she promised them a treat once they had begun.

She sent them to fetch their work-boxes while she arranged chairs near the schoolroom window to catch the light. She helped them choose their silks, put the material in embroidery frames and watched them make a start.

Sarah's stitches were far too large. Twice Belinda made her unpick the cross-stitch on the letter 'A' but eventually she decided to let Sarah continue rather than argue. Kitty's stitching was neater but she worked listlessly.

"Now that you have begun, I will read to you," Belinda said.

"Nothing improving, I hope," growled Kitty.

"I thought perhaps a novel," Belinda said artlessly, and laughed to herself when at once they cheered up.

"Sir Charles Grandison!" Sarah clasped her hands together, "that is beyond anything great!"

"It is indeed, but I have a new novel given me by my aunt as a parting present. It's called The Orphan of the Rhine."

"That sounds splendid, let's hope it's full of horrors," cried Kitty. "Do read it to us, Miss Farrington."

Belinda fetched it. "I'll read on condition you sew a little faster, Kitty, and that you make your stitches smaller, Sarah."

"Oh I will," said Sarah fervently. "You are a trump, Miss Farrington. Miss Turner, our last governess, was excessively disapproving of novels and we love them."

Everything went smoothly from then on. The samplers progressed and the girls shuddered happily at the harrowing trials of the heroine. Towards noon, they were interrupted by Mrs. Sheldon.

"Miss Farrington, now that the rain has stopped, I'm going shopping and would like to take the girls with me."

Belinda had got the girls working well and had won their approval: enough progress had been made for the day. She smiled dutifully and sent them to change their dresses.

"You may have the afternoon to yourself, Miss Farrington, and do me a kindness at the same time." She handed Belinda a basket of camellias and asked her to take them to the village church and arrange them.

"It's the church's patronal festival on Sunday and I promised the vicar some of my choicest blooms. As a clergyman's daughter, my dear, you will know just how to go on. Flower arranging is a peaceful task; it gives one time for quiet reflection."

As Belinda walked to the church, she thought that Mrs. Sheldon was a woman who frequently put her own comfort and pleasure before all else. If any task were disagreeable to her, she got someone else to do it while making it seem as if she were bestowing a favour. But Belinda didn't mind: she was pleased to be on her own for once and out in the fresh air, inhaling the scents of the rain washed countryside.

Her brisk pace carried her quickly to the church and she slipped in through the heavy door at the back. The interior was cool and dim and brought back memories of times she had decorated the church for Papa. A small sigh of regret escaped her as she laid down the basket and began to sort the blooms.

As she snipped the stalks, readying the flowers for the large vase in front of the pulpit, she began to consider the conclusions she had come to about the various members of the Sheldon family. She was gradually gaining Kitty and Sarah's confidence and their behaviour was improving; she got on well with Mark who was sympathetic and treated her in a flattering way. But it was upon Clive that her thoughts chiefly dwelt.

She was attracted to him: his magnetic personality affected her powerfully. His unfair scoldings still rankled but when he was charming as he had been at nuncheon yesterday, she found him irresistible. But, she told herself severely, she must not dream about him; he must be destined for someone more eligible than a penniless governess. She couldn't help hoping that it would not be Miss Isabella Hallingbury.

Her musings were disturbed by the squeak of the door hinges. She peeped round the pulpit and a swarm of butterflies seemed to rise in her stomach as she recognised the shining hessians, the pale yellow pantaloons, olive green coat and snowy stock.

Clive!

It was as if her thoughts had conjured him. In a moment of agitation, she stepped back into the shadow where he would not see her.

He strode up the aisle and went to the vestry door and began to speak in a low voice to someone inside. Belinda was startled; she had thought herself alone in the church and wondered to whom he was speaking. Although she knew she should not do so, she tried to hear what he was saying but the low murmur made the words indistinct.

After a few moments of conversation, Clive turned and walked back looking neither to left nor right. When she was sure he had left the church, she came out of hiding and resumed her flower arranging, wondering why she had instinctively avoided a meeting. Was it because she had been thinking forbidden thoughts about him and feared that somehow they would show up on her face?

The afternoon sun shining through the west window cast a patchwork of jewel colours onto the tiled floor and suffused the camellias with rainbow hues. She smiled contentedly: Mrs. Sheldon was right, flower arranging was a soothing task. She felt at peace with the world.

A little later on, when her arrangement was finished and she was preparing to go, the heavy door creaked again. She looked round. It was Jevons, Clive's wizened little manservant. This time she did not hide.

Jevons jumped when he saw Belinda. "You here, Miss?"

"I have finished doing the flowers and I was just leaving." She picked up her basket and shawl and walked down the aisle.

As he held the door open for her, Jevons explained himself. "Just going in to speak to the verger."

Belinda nodded and walked past. When she got to the lych-gate she realised to her annoyance, that she had left her scissors behind. She retraced her steps, her soft shoes making no noise, and pushed the door open. She was astonished at the sight that met her eyes. Jevons was kneeling in front of the altar. Its embroidered frontal cloth was thrown back and he was removing a small barrel from the space below the communion table.

Belinda felt sure this was something she was not supposed to see and turned to go but in her perturbation, she dropped her basket with a clatter that echoed in the vast space of the nave.

Jevons spun round, an expression of horror on his face. Seeing Belinda, he relaxed. "My heart! It's you, Miss. You gave me quite a turn! I thought it was that nosy riding officer."

"I came back for my scissors," Belinda explained, hurrying to the pulpit. She found them and picked them up quickly.

Jevons grinned. "That's all right, then. I'm just doing something for the Gentlemen. Mum's the word, eh, Miss?"

Belinda, furious at being involved, nodded, scuttled out of the church and fled back to Park Place. As she hurried along, she thought about what she had seen. She was shocked that contraband was hidden in the church and surprised that a respectable upper servant like Jevons should be involved with the smugglers...

She stopped. The reason struck her like a blow. If Clive was indeed the Master-smuggler, what could be more natural than that his valet would also take part in the trade? She thought she saw the pattern: Clive had been making arrangements with the verger and then sent Jevons to fetch the barrel. She was bitterly disappointed to have her vague suspicion about Clive made solid.

She spent an uncomfortable evening; the knowledge she had acquired made her feel unable to look Clive in the face. She spent a restless night wondering what to do. It was not her business what her employer's family did, yet smuggling was breaking the law. She was not prepared to betray Clive to Yardley, yet she felt guilty about keeping silent. There was no-one in whom she could confide or ask for advice. How she longed for Papa with his clear-cut thinking and strong moral precepts.

Next morning, by the lake when she was supervising the despised water colours which were being attempted again, she found her confidant. Mark strolled down and exchanged greetings with her. He teased his sisters about their pictures which infuriated them, then he asked Belinda if she would take a turn round the lake with him.

Kitty and Sarah giggled as she blushingly agreed. Once out of earshot of the painters, she said,

"I'm glad of this opportunity to talk with you, Mr. Mark. I have a problem and would like your advice."

"Only too happy to be of service, Miss Farrington."

Belinda began by telling him what Yardley had said of the three senior Sheldons. Mark was furious. "Well if that don't beat the Dutch! What a fool that riding officer is!"

"I didn't regard it," Belinda hastened to assure him. "I thought it was nonsense until yesterday." She told him about seeing Clive and Jevons in the church.

"Jevons is sapskull! It is true that half the servants in the house and stables are in the Gentlemen's pay but he had no cause to blab to you. I'll lay a monkey Clive doesn't know his man's involved and wouldn't like it above half if he did. Clive is straight as a die and goes in for pound dealing. You surely can't believe he would have anything to do with smuggling?"

Belinda shook her head doubtfully. She was not convinced but his spirited defence of his brother gave her a very good opinion of Mark. Then she spoke of her other cause for concern.

"It seems very wrong to hide contraband liquor in a church."

Mark grinned. "It's not regarded so here. The smugglers use the dark nights when they come over from France to dodge the patrols, but the pack trains need the moon. Between the dark and the moon the goods must be hidden—farmers leave their barn doors ajar and in return get tea or a keg of brandy on their doorstep. Probably the vicar gets the same for allowing the Gentlemen to use the church."

Belinda found this hard to believe. "I'm sure my papa would not have done so."

Mark shrugged. "Needs must when the devil drives the box. All sorts of curious hidey holes are used. The time between the dark and the light is the time of greatest danger for the smugglers for it is then that the riding officer works hardest. Suspicion is no good, Yardley has plenty of that. The culprits must be caught in possession of run goods. The fines are heavy—ten pounds for receiving contraband and fifty pounds for supplying it and the smugglers either go to prison or are pressed into the navy."

"How dreadful! So, you don't think Mr. Clive is involved?"

"Certainly not and you can discount Papa so that leaves me. I collect you don't think I'm the Master-smuggler?" He gave her his winning, blue-eyed smile.

"No indeed." She smiled back warmly. "How could I think so?"

She was confident about Mark but not perfectly sure about Clive.

* * *

When the day of Isabella's picnic came it confounded the pessimists: the weather was fine. She arrived at Park Place looking important with baskets of food prepared by her mother's cook. When everyone was assembled, she announced that their destination was Blythburgh, a pretty village on the coast.

"It has a fascinating church," she told them with a beaming smile, "with all manner of historical associations."

"Sounds gloomy," said Mark who couldn't resist teasing Isabella.

"Boring, more like," said Kitty rudely, earning frowns from her mother and Belinda, "I hate improving outings."

"Don't be disagreeable, Kitty." Mrs. Sheldon spoke sharply. "Isabella has planned this as a treat."

"And I am sure we shall enjoy it," Clive said smoothing Isabella's ruffled feathers.

She bridled. "Don't forget, Clive, I'm to go in your curricle."

"Don't forget, Isabella," said Sarah sweetly sidling up to her, her eyes gleaming with mischief, "I'm to ride bodkin between you and Clive."

Belinda was hard put to it not to laugh. Isabella had ignored Belinda on arrival but she did not mind for she knew she was looking her best. Annoyed by Isabella's remarks about her costly shawl, Belinda had deliberately chosen an expensive outfit for the occasion, a rose wool pelisse over a buff silk dress and a bonnet of natural straw trimmed with roses to match the pelisse. She hoped very much that Isabella would disapprove.

Isabella was wearing pale green muslin with dark green floss trimmings and a rose patterned Norwich shawl. A tiny pale green hat swathed with dark green veiling completed her ensemble.

"Her shawl is not as pretty as yours," Sarah whispered loyally to Belinda as they waited in the hall while the curricle and barouche were brought round.

* * *

Belinda enjoyed the drive sitting between Kitty and Mark. The sky was cloudless, the sun was shining and the countryside was clad in its fresh spring greenery. Her first sight was of Blythburgh church set up on a bluff, the grey dressed stone standing out against a clear blue sky impressed her.

The curricle arrived first and as the barouche pulled up, Isabella bustled over and began to organise in a way calculated to make everyone wish to do the opposite of what she suggested. Luckily she was too thick-skinned to notice the hostility.

"We'll look at the church first before our alfresco feast," she began, taking out a small pocket book. "I have made a note of what we should particularly look for."

"Been swotting up in all the guide books, have you Isabella? I should never have taken you for a blue-stocking," Mark said.

"I am not that, Mark," she said severely. "You gentlemen pride yourselves on your superior knowledge but I think it is the duty of a lady to be well-informed to add tone to conversation. Don't you agree, Clive?"

Clive was trying not to laugh. "Definitely," he said burying his face in his handkerchief as if to arrest a sneeze.

Isabella began to lecture them about a battle that took place at Blythburgh in the seventh century. Sarah quickly became bored and Kitty mutinous.

"I think we should go inside," Clive said, anxious to prevent war from breaking out between Isabella and his sisters.

"Pray pay particular attention to the north door," said bossy Isabella, "where we shall see the imprint of the devil's red-hot talons."

This captured the interest of the two girls but caused Clive to look at Isabella askance. "Come now, Bella, that is moonshine."

"According to my notebook," said Isabella disregarding this interruption and bending her golden head over her notes, "he came to the church in a thunder storm one Sunday in August 1577. He scorched the people, struck the bells from the steeple and rushed from the church leaving his hand mark on the door."

"Flummery!" said Mark. "You don't really believe that Banbury tale, do you Isabella?"

Both the men were scornful but the girls loved it.

"I believe it." Sarah's eyes were round. "Tell me more

about the devil, Isabella."

Isabella smiled complacently. "After that, he flew off to Bungay changing into a huge black dog on the way."

Mark burst out laughing but Kitty was impressed.

"Black Shuck!" she breathed in a tone of awe.

"What is Black Shuck?" Belinda was intrigued; this was like something from one of Mrs. Radcliffe's novels.

"And you a governess!" said Isabella scornfully. "I thought everyone knew about Black Shuck."

"Not unless you grew up in these parts," Clive said. To Isabella's annoyance, he defended Belinda and turned to her to explain.

"Black Shuck is the ghost dog of East Anglia, the bogy of Suffolk nurseries and the spectre that keeps folk indoors on dark nights. It's my belief that tales of Black Shuck are put about by smugglers to keep people away from their hiding places."

Belinda was startled. She looked hard at Clive, amazed that he should speak so coolly about smugglers. She began to wonder if her suspicion of him could be mistaken.

"Come," Mark said to his sisters, "you'll never be satisfied until you've seen the devil's mark: we'd better take a look."

They were disappointed. There were some scratches but they did not find them convincing.

"I told you it was flummery," Mark said.

Isabella led them into the church. "Notice, if you please, the bench ends which depict the seven deadly sins."

"Oh Lor', more improvement," Kitty grumbled.

"Do try to be a little more gracious," said Belinda in an undervoice, "Miss Hallingbury is doing her best to entertain us."

Belinda was enchanted by the interior of the church. She turned to Clive, her face alight with pleasure. "How light and airy it is, and those beams—such a lovely soft shade of grey, almost silver."

Clive smiled back. "It's the action of the salt air on the

oak," he said. "The soft colours that decorate the bosses also owe their subtlety to the sea air fading them—they were probably startlingly bright when the church was first built."

Belinda nodded, admiring the carved roof bosses fashioned like angels holding shields. Their rigid curls were gilded. Each wing feather was delicately carved and their expressions were cool and serene.

She said reverently, "It is quite, quite beautiful."

Clive was pleased. "It is my favourite of the many lovely churches in the county. I'm glad you like it too."

Isabella saw them together and bustled up jealously and told them sharply to look at the carvings. Clive made a face like a naughty boy caught stealing jam and moved along with Isabella.

Belinda would have liked to examine the bench ends but she only had time to notice Slander with his slit tongue like the child's rhyme—'Tell tale tit, your tongue shall be slit,'—and Sloth, a little man still in bed, too lazy to get up, before she realised that Kitty and Sarah were bored and looking about for mischief.

Regretfully, she decided it was her duty to distract them and she told Mark she would take them for a walk.

He nodded and whispered, "I'll stay with Clive and Isabella, we don't want her to get him on his own, do we?" He winked at her wickedly.

Belinda suggested to the girls that they should walk down to look at the sea. They began to stroll beside a grassy bank but they had not gone far when they heard mournful whimpering.

Sarah ran up the bank and looked over it. She called back, her voice full of distress, "Oh Miss Farrington, there's an animal caught in a snare. What shall we do?"

Belinda scrambled up the bank and joined her to look down into the ditch. "Oh, how cruel! It's a dog, I must go and see if I can help it."

Without giving a thought to her elegant attire, Belinda

scrambled down into the ditch and approached the trapped
animal, a large, black sheepdog. From its condition, she
guessed it had been there some time. Its coat was matted with
mud, its eyes were wild and its tongue lolled thirstily. The
cruel wire loop had cut deep into its leg which was bleeding.

"Don't touch it, it's Black Shuck!" shrieked Kitty
dramatically, "Don't go near it, Miss Farrington, it'll bring
you your death!"

"Don't be such a wet-goose, Kitty. Go and call your
brothers; see if one of them has a pocket knife."

Kitty shook her head but Sarah ran to do her bidding.
Belinda moved slowly towards the dog, murmuring gentle
nothings as she drew near. It permitted her to approach, but
when she tried to touch its leg, it growled. Patiently, she
stroked and gentled it until she won its trust.

Soon, Mark, Clive and Isabella came up, led by Sarah.
Kitty, convinced it was Black Shuck, turned her back and
refused to have anything to do with the proceedings.

"Oh, how horrid!" cried Isabella. "But it's only a farm dog,
don't trouble with it. Come to nuncheon."

Clive gave her a look of disgust. "We can't abandon an
animal in pain. You have your nuncheon if you like. I'm
going to assist Miss Farrington."

He jumped into the ditch but when he tried to help, the
dog would have none of it and growled fiercely.

"Pass me your pocket knife, if you please, Mr. Clive,"
Belinda said; "he seems to trust me. I'll cut the wire."

"You'll never do that but you will find the wire is fastened
to a wooden peg; you'll have better luck digging that out." He
handed her the knife.

Talking soothingly to the dog, Belinda found the peg and
began to grub out the earth round it. The peg was difficult to
remove, but at last she pulled it free. The dog struggled to its
feet but yelped when it put the injured leg to the ground.

"We'll have to carry him," Clive said. "I'm afraid you must
take the front as he thinks I'm an ogre, I'll take his hind

quarters. Take him to my curricle and we'll try to reunite him with his owner."

They scrambled up the bank with the unwieldy dog carried between them. As they made for the curricle, Isabella called to them.

"Where are you going? You're not going to spoil my picnic for the sake of a filthy animal are you?"

Clive looked at her coldly. "Try to have a little compassion, Isabella, this dog is badly hurt. Miss Farrington and I will deal with the matter. The rest of you can picnic and Mark can bring you home later."

As they manoeuvred the dog into the curricle and settled him with his head in Belinda's lap, they heard Isabella say petulantly, "This is the outside of enough. I knew it was a mistake to let that wretched governess come—she has spoiled everything."

As they drove away, Clive said, "I'm sorry you should have heard that. Isabella is wretchedly selfish, she lacks manners as well as compassion."

"But what she said is true: I have spoiled her picnic."

"You were splendid, Miss Farrington. Few ladies of my acquaintance would have acted so boldly, made so little fuss and showed so little regard for their clothes—you have ruined a very pretty dress."

Belinda glowed. "What does that signify, sir, as long as the dog is all right?"

As Clive drove at a brisk pace, the dog looked up at Belinda trustingly. Before long, they saw coming towards them a man in a shepherd's smock looking anxiously from side to side, calling and whistling. The exhausted dog pricked its ears.

Observing this, Clive said, "I think we've found his master.'

The reunion was joyous. The shepherd explained that he had missed Old Shep the night before but had thought the dog would come home later. As he did not, the shepherd had resumed his search and had been looking for him since first light. He lifted the dog gently and draped him across his shoulder, thanking them over and over again and assuring them Shep would get the best of care.

After the shepherd and the dog had gone, Clive said, "Do you mind if we don't go back? I've lost my appetite for food and for Isabella's company."

"No indeed, and I am not fit to be seen. I should prefer to return to Park Place."

Belinda's heart sang. If the truth were told, she did not care where she went as long as she was with Clive. She would have gone to the ends of the earth with him. He was a splendid man: no one who showed such concern for a dog could possibly be the Master-smuggler.

How could she have been so bird-witted as to think he was?

Chapter Five

The harum-scarum boys were due to arrive home the day after Isabella's picnic. The girls were excited and were only working half-heartedly on their samplers. As they sewed, they talked. Having exhausted their speculation as to why their brothers had been rusticated, they turned to discussing the previous day's events. Much as Belinda deplored gossip, she found it difficult to stop them chatting about Isabella's bad behaviour.

"I think Clive's eyes are opened now," Kitty said, "her attitude to that poor dog revolted him."

"Let that be a warning to you," Belinda said lightly, "never do anything that may give a gentleman a disgust of you. Modesty and compassion are what gentlemen admire."

At that moment, they heard the sound of wheels on the gravel.

Sarah jumped up from her chair shrieking, "The boys! They're here, they're here!"

Belinda rapped on the table with her scissors and tried to look stern. "Try for a little conduct, if you please!"

Sarah sobered instantly.

Kitty said with exaggerated politeness, "Please, Miss Farrington, may we lay our work aside and go to greet them?"

"Do say yes," added Sarah anxiously.

Belinda hadn't the heart to refuse. "Very well, but don't run. Remember, you are young ladies, not wild animals."

Eyes sparkling, the girls hurried from the schoolroom. Belinda followed sedately behind. She had heard so much about Will and Simon that she was curious to see them. She was expecting fiends in human shape and was agreeably surprised by her first impression.

In the hall, surrounded by boxes, bags, bats, racquets and fishing rods, two young gentlemen were greeting their mother. Clive and Mark, not wanting to miss the fun, lounged in the background.

Kitty and Sarah erupted into the hall.

"Will, how splendid you look!" said Kitty bouncing up to the elder boy and planting a kiss on his cheek.

"Something's wrong with Kitty's eye sight if she thinks that waistcoat splendid," said Clive, his lips twitching in a way Belinda was beginning to recognise.

"That's all you know," said the waistcoat's proud possessor hotly. "This colour's all the crack in town."

"Is it indeed, or did your tailor tell you that?" Mark was grinning.

"He must have seen Will coming. I dare swear he was glad to get rid of it," Clive agreed, his eyes twinkling. "Aping the dandy set, Will?"

Will Sheldon blushed and Belinda, unused to family teasing, felt sorry for him. He was tall for sixteen. His brown hair was a modish tumble of curls, but it was his clothes that made Belinda stare. His coat was nipped in tightly at the waist, and the tops of the sleeves were puffed up almost to his ears. The stiffly starched points of his shirt collar were so high and his stock so tight that his head was held rigid and he had to turn his whole body to see what was beside him. The offending waistcoat was a startling shade of puce. Belinda realised that Clive was right: Will wished to be considered a dandy but she did not think his outrageous clothes gave him anything like the air of distinction that Clive's severe, beautifully tailored ones did.

Will glared at his brothers but smiled broadly as Sarah threw herself at him.

"Mind my cravat, Bratling," he said amiably.

Then Sarah threw herself upon Simon. The younger boy was carelessly dressed in loose, country clothes. Straight brown hair hung round a cheerful, grubby face and round his neck he wore a spotted neckerchief as if he were going ratting.

"What ho, little 'un," he said to Sarah. "Ain't it famous that we're home?"

"Don't gloat," warned Mrs. Sheldon, "Papa is waiting to see you so you can explain your rustication." She introduced them to Belinda.

They both bowed and Simon gave Belinda an infectious grin.

Kitty whispered to Will, "Come to the schoolroom after you've seen Papa, we're dying to hear about it too."

As the boys disappeared into Mr. Sheldon's book room, Belinda took the girls upstairs again.

"Need we carry on with our sewing?" Kitty begged.

Belinda shook her head. She could see no work would be done today; the harum-scarum boys would be the centre of attention. She would not have admitted it to the girls, but she too was consumed with curiosity and longed to hear their story.

It was not long before the boys came into the schoolroom, closely followed by Clive and Mark who, it appeared were as anxious to hear their story as their sisters.

"I'm glad that's over," said Simon throwing himself into a chair in the schoolroom. "What a pi-jaw we had from Papa!"

"One of his worst," agreed Will draping himself artistically against the mantelpiece.

"Well," said Mark impatiently, "let's hear all about this rebellion or whatever it was."

The young Sheldons were crammed into the schoolroom. It was the first time Belinda had seen them all together. She noticed the family likeness that linked them as well as their individual differences. She could see they relished each other's company: she was beginning to realise that the teasing which had at first appeared to her to be hostility and rudeness was, in fact, affection. She reflected wistfully that there was much that she, as an only child, had missed.

"It wasn't a rebellion, it was a barring out," said Will.

"It was the most famous thing." Simon's eyes were sparkling.

Between them, Will and Simon told the story using so much schoolboy slang that on several occasions, Belinda had to apply to Mark for interpretation.

It had begun, they said, when the boys of Westminster, tired of the frequency of the Headmaster's floggings, set fire to the birch and block, then barricaded themselves in the Upper Classroom.

"We stayed there for three days," Will said.

"What did you do about food?" Clive asked.

"We let down a basket on a rope from a back window and had bub and grub sent up," Simon told him.

Will continued the story. Every time the masters tried to break in, he said, the boys repelled them by hurling missiles. Finally, one over enthusiastic young man fired a sporting gun and shot a master in the arm.

"The fat was in the fire then," Will said, "the Bagwig called out the militia and sent for a magistrate to read the Riot Act."

Mark whispered that the Bagwig was the headmaster but Belinda took little notice, finding the idea of the militia and the Riot Act very alarming. But the Sheldons seemed unperturbed and were all listening avidly, eyes aglow.

"Oh, how exciting. What happened next?" Kitty asked.

Simon grinned. "We knew the game was up then so we shinnyed down a rope at the back and piked on the bean."

"That means they ran away," Mark told Belinda, grinning as broadly as his younger brother.

"Of course we had to go back, but not before we'd kicked up some larks in the town. That's when the Head declared an amnesty and sent us all home for six weeks to cool off," Will finished.

"Bravo!" cried Sarah.

Clive seemed about to echo this sentiment but suddenly he remembered his age and frowned. "It sounds thoroughly irresponsible to me. What started it all off, apart from this weak, lily-livered dislike of flogging?"

"We got to talking about rebellion. You know how we're locked into the Long Dormitory at nights? Well, when we aren't drinking and dicing we talk; the French Revolution—Tom Paine—all that stuff. Times are changing, you know. We decided that we boys ought to have a say in the conduct of the school."

Mark burst out laughing. "Impudent puppies!"

"No wonder the Bagwig flogged you," Clive said, "you're a set of dangerous radicals! I never thought I'd hear a brother of mine preaching revolution."

Mark was still laughing. "The Rights of Man, my dear Will, not boys, Tom Paine said nothing about the rights of boys."

"That's what the Bagwig said!" Simon was much struck that his brother and his Headmaster should share an opinion.

"The real trigger was the news that the Prime Minister had been murdered," Will said. "When we heard that, we thought the revolution was starting and didn't want to miss it. That and our grievances about the birch and block were what started it."

"Revolution indeed!" snorted Clive. "Mr. Spencer Perceval was shot by a madman who has been carried off to Bedlam. Lord Liverpool has taken over the government and will certainly see there is no revolution."

"That's all you know," Simon retorted truculently. "There's a deal of revolutionary talk in London, I can tell you. The other night, some of the fellows broke out of the dorm. I went too, thinking we were going to a boozing-ken with females and dancing. It was a sell, a complete take-in. They went to a meeting of a set of jaw-me-deads called the London Corresponding Society who did nothing but prose on about machine breaking. I've never heard such boring stuff."

Mark couldn't stop laughing. "No need to worry about him, Clive; he plainly prefers petticoats to politics, if you'll excuse the expression, Miss Farrington."

Belinda smiled weakly. She didn't understand the politics but she thought Clive was taking a very harsh attitude which was confirmed when he said, "I think the Bagwig was right to flog you. A flogging all round instead of rustication would have been my solution."

"That's cruel," Belinda said. "I am persuaded you did right to protest about such things, Will."

"There you are quite wrong, Miss Farrington," Clive said severely. "You simply don't understand. Flogging and bullying toughen the boys. It happened in my day and it hasn't hurt Mark or me. Why, when we were at Westminster, there was one fight in which a fellow killed another with a penknife: I thought that was going too far, but in my opinion, if it wasn't for the practices of the dormitory at Westminster and the quarterdeck of a man o' war, we should become a nation of simpering dandies."

Belinda bit her lip. How could Clive speak with such shocking callousness? After hearing such sentiments, she began to revise her good opinion of him. A man who believed in such things could easily be the Master-smuggler.

* * *

Belinda tossed restlessly. It was a hot night—too hot for sleep. After a brilliant June day the atmosphere was sultry, the still air was heavy with the scent of new mown hay. The moon was shining brightly and it was a shaft of moonlight stealing through a gap in the curtains that woke her. She got out of bed to adjust the curtains and shut out the bright light.

As she did so, she looked down into the stable yard and was arrested by the sight of a line of sturdy ponies leaving the yard. Their feet were tied up in sacking to deaden the sound of their tread, and bulky bundles were slung across their withers.

The smugglers' pack train!

She shivered, wondering if Yardley and his men were out there somewhere, lying in wait. If so, she feared there would be an affray for the men leading the ponies were armed with cudgels. Her thoughts flew to Clive until she remembered with relief that he had gone to visit friends.

But had he? Was not this exactly what had happened at the time of the last run? Did he "go to visit friends" as a cover for far more sinister activities? And why was she concerned for Clive's safety? Was it because of the extraordinary feelings he evoked in her?

A few days ago while she was still holding aloof from him, shocked at his heartless pronouncements to the boys, his hand had brushed hers as he politely handed her a book that had fallen to the schoolroom floor. The sensation caused by his touch had startled her: tingling seemed to leap from his hand to hers. Then he had smiled at her and her bones seemed to liquefy.

It had been strangely disconcerting. She knew she ought to deny his attraction for her for two reasons: firstly because no connection was possible owing to the inequality of their positions and their fortunes, and secondly, there were times when she disapproved of him strongly and felt sure he was the Master-smuggler.

Yet she found it hard to deny her feeling for Clive: it was different from anything she had known before. It was not the schoolgirl's hero-worship she had felt for George, it was not the easy, comradely affection she felt for Mark, it was something dark and disturbing but exhilarating. Her heart yearned for him but her head told her to keep him at arm's length.

She sighed and went back to bed. Even with the curtains drawn to exclude the moonlight, Belinda, tormented by thoughts of her love for Clive, spent a restless night.

* * *

Now Will and Simon were home, breakfast was set out in the dining room and Belinda and the girls were expected to join the rest of the family. Next morning when they went down, Mr. Sheldon, Clive and Mark had already gone, but Mrs. Sheldon and the harum-scarum boys were still at the table. Mrs. Sheldon was sipping tea and eating fingers of toast, watching with amazement the huge quantities of steak and eggs her younger sons devoured.

Sarah slipped into a seat next to Simon who was again wearing his knotted neckerchief which Belinda had heard him tell Sarah was called a Belcher after a famous prize fighter. Kitty took a place next to Will who looked more comfortable and natural in his country clothes than in the ones in which he had arrived from school.

"Famous news," Simon said to Sarah. "The Gentlemen dished the excisemen last night. It seems there were two pack trains—one with the goods which got clean away and another, laden with bales of hay. That was the one the excisemen found! Ain't it capital? I'll wager the riding officer feels down-pin this morning."

"Simon," chided his mother, "you shouldn't wish anyone ill fortune. There will be sore heads among the villagers today, I fear. I understand they gave battle when they were challenged."

"I wish I had been there," said Will, "I like nothing better than a mill."

Mrs. Sheldon looked pained. "You shouldn't speak about smuggling or fighting in front of ladies, Will. I know many gentlemen take a keen interest in pugilism, but I don't wish to hear about it."

"Sorry Mamma," Will said and grinned at Simon.

Belinda wondered whether it had been the true or the false pack train she had seen from her bedroom window. She felt a little sorry for Yardley; he would, as Simon had suggested, be feeling depressed this morning.

After breakfast, Kitty asked Belinda if they could go riding.

"You need not come, Miss Farrington, if you do not wish to. We shall be quite safe with Will and Simon."

Belinda did not consider the harum-scarum boys suitable chaperones.

"I should enjoy a ride," she said, "an outing will do us all good. Go and change into your riding habits. I will join you in the stables directly."

On her way downstairs, dressed in her dark green habit frogged with black braid like a rifleman's tunic with a becoming helmet shaped hat with mallard feathers curling over the crown, she met Mrs. Sheldon coming up. The habit was part of her trousseau and had been chosen to compliment George. Miss Isabella Hallingbury would have thought it far too dashing for a governess and Belinda hoped Mrs. Sheldon would not think so too. But she need not have worried.

"How charming you look, Miss Farrington. I am glad to see you are to accompany the children: I feared there was mischief afoot when I heard they planned to ride out in a foursome."

"My thoughts exactly, ma'am. I shall endeavour to see they all behave."

Belinda was looking forward to the ride. She was not worried that she would disgrace herself in her charges' eyes, for she had ridden a great deal in Yorkshire accompanying her papa, and had light hands and a good seat.

When she rounded the corner of the house she was horrified at the sight that met her eyes. Will, without his coat which Simon was holding, was squared up to one of the stable boys, his fists bunched, ready to fight. This was bad enough but even more shocking was the sight of the girls who were behaving like Billingsgate fishwives, jumping up and down shouting encouragement in an unfamiliar jargon that Belinda took to be boxing cant.

"Plant him a facer!" shrieked Kitty.

"Draw his cork!" cried Sarah.

"Tap his claret!" urged Simon.

Will and Tom were circling warily, fists revolving, their faces an angry red. Belinda disapproved of fighting and wanted to remonstrate with Will but her first concern was to remove the girls from the scene.

"Kitty, Sarah! Come away at once." She took hold of their arms.

"It's a mill, Miss Farrington, a fight! You couldn't make us miss it," Sarah said.

"Indeed I could. Into the house at once and go straight to the schoolroom."

"Go on Will, it'll be bellows to mend with him in a trice." Simon egged his brother on as Will jabbed out, landing a hard blow on the stable boy's body.

"A wisty-castor!" Sarah shouted from the other side of the yard as she and Kitty retreated at snail's pace. Belinda's palm itched to smack them.

"The little 'un's game as a pebble," Simon said to Belinda with a grin. "Knows all the boxing cant."

"And I collect you taught her," Belinda said sharply. "You should be ashamed."

But Simon was too interested in the fight to care. As Will landed a blow on his opponent's face he called, "Well done, Will. A flush hit. That'll have shifted his ivories."

Belinda was revolted. She darted forward and stepped between the fighters, trying to part them. "I forbid you..." she began.

But it was too late: Will had already wound himself up for his haymaker when she stepped in. It connected with Belinda who was instantly felled.

As she lay on the ground, Will stood over her looking down. He was appalled. "Miss Farrington! I'm so sorry."

At this moment Clive swept into the stable yard driving his curricle. Taking in the scene at a glance, he leaped down, threw his reins to a groom and strode over to Belinda and scooped her up from the cobbles.

"You are a constant surprise to me, Miss Farrington," he

murmured as he carried her towards the house. "I fear you are
going to have what is known in boxing circles as a shiner. I
shall bathe it for you."

Belinda was dazed and in pain but not entirely unhappy to
be held against Clive's chest with his strong arms round her,
although she realised how foolish she must appear in his eyes.

"Sir," she began.

He interrupted. "Please don't explain, Miss Farrington. I
am having a perfectly delightful time inventing stories to
account for your entry into pugilism."

In spite of his promise, it was Mrs. Sheldon and her
dresser, Miss Lally, who attended to Belinda's eye. Mrs.
Sheldon was outraged at his suggestion that beefsteak would
be better than the witch hazel she was using.

"That may be all very well for gentlemen but not for a
lady," she said and sent him about his business.

Belinda lay in a darkened room and dozed for a while.
When she had recovered her equilibrium she felt guilty at
taking her rest when the house was so busy. She was perfectly
well although her face ached, so she got up. Looking in her
mirror, she was taken aback at the hideous bruising round her
eye and when she had dressed, she covered it with a scarf tied
into a narrow strip.

Downstairs she found the family in the drawing room.
Mark and Clive were chatting to their mamma while the
younger children played a noisy game of lottery tickets.

"A lady pirate," crowed Mark taking in her bandaged eye,
"or is it a lady prize fighter?"

"Don't tease," said Mrs. Sheldon. She signalled to Will
who immediately left the game and came over and offered
Belinda a handsome apology.

"It is of no consequence." She forgave him with a smile.

"People who interfere in the quarrels of others must expect
such retribution, must they not, Miss Farrington?" Clive said.
His tone was severe but he smiled at her. "I hope you are
feeling better?"

She coloured, wondering what he meant. "Much better, thank you, sir."

Then Belinda noticed that Clive too had been in the wars, because he had a large court plaster on his forehead. Her heart sank. She immediately concluded he had earned it the previous night in the fight between the smugglers and the excisemen.

Belinda dared not ask him about it, and it was not until the next day that she discovered in a roundabout way how he came to be injured. She and the girls were sitting in the schoolroom sewing. Sarah reported indignantly that Will had been beaten by Papa.

"I think it's so unfair; he said Will shouldn't have fought with a social inferior, but Will doesn't think of Tom like that. He and Tom were always together before Will went off to school; bird nesting, climbing trees and running foot races. Tom was Will's particular friend."

Belinda said, "But you must see what your papa means; village boys and the sons of great houses play together when they are young, but as they grow there are distinctions and obligations. You girls were allowed to run wild with the boys when you were little but now you are young ladies, so very different behaviour is expected of you."

"More's the pity," Kitty said morosely. "I should have thought Papa would understand about fighting. The mill Clive went to yesterday was between Sir Marmaduke Dereham and a coal heaver. Clive told Will they were perfectly matched for height and weight but you could hardly call that a fight between social equals."

"Clive went to a prize fight?" Belinda said in surprise.

"That's where he got the cut on his head," Sarah said knowingly. "It seems that some of the gentlemen weren't satisfied with the result and fell to fighting among themselves. Clive was hit trying to part two of his friends—just like you when you tried to separate Will and Tom."

Now Belinda understood Clive's remark about those who

interfered and her heart lifted. Although she disapproved of fisticuffs, she was overjoyed that Clive had not been fighting the excisemen.

Kitty said, "I wonder what Will and Tom were fighting about?"

Simon's cheerful, untidy head appeared round the schoolroom door. "Would you really like to know?"

"Of course we would, do tell," Sarah said eagerly as she grabbed him and pulled him in.

"Try to guess," he said perching on the edge of the table, swinging his leg.

"A guessing game," cried Kitty. "I dote on them. You must allow us three questions before we guess."

"Carlton House to a Charlie's shelter you won't get it," Simon said with a complacent grin.

"Is it to do with a female?" Kitty asked.

"No."

"Is it to do with one of our brothers?" Sarah enquired.

"Yes. Only one more question."

"Which brother?" asked Kitty.

"Mark. Now you must guess."

"That's easy," Kitty said. "If it's about Mark it must be about one of his lights o' love."

"Kitty!" Belinda was shocked. "What a vulgar remark. Mr. Mark is not like that."

"Much you know!" muttered Kitty.

"You're wrong, Kitty," Simon said. "It wasn't about one of his flirts."

"What was it then?" Sarah said. "We give up."

"Do you want to try, Miss Farrington?" Simon offered.

Belinda put on her best governess's expression. "No thank you, Simon. I cannot approve of this game, it is little more than disguised gossip and unsuitable for young ladies and gentlemen." This was unfair of her because she did want to know.

"I'll tell you anyway," Simon said with a grin. "They got

into an argument when Tom said Mark was the Master-smuggler. Will said, 'Gammon!' Tom said it was true: Will called him a liar and the fight began."

"I cannot approve of fighting but I do see Will's point," Belinda said. "It's ridiculous to think Mr. Mark would have anything to do with smuggling."

"Do you know who the Master-smuggler is?" Sarah asked her brother.

Simon shook his head vigorously. "Not I and I'd rather not know—it wouldn't be healthy."

"That's enough of that," said Belinda. "You know your mamma forbade you to talk about smuggling and fighting in front of ladies. And I should remind you, Simon, that this is lesson time. The girls have to make progress with their samplers. Either you must sit down quietly with a book or I must ask you to leave."

Simon grinned. "I think I'll go down to the lake and see if I can catch a fish. See you all at dinner."

Kitty glowered at her brother's retreating back. "It's not fair. They've been sent home because they were bad, but they are allowed to do as they like: we've been good and we're cooped up here sewing."

"Whatever gave you the idea that life is fair, Kitty?" Belinda said. But she took pity on them and sent them out to enjoy the fresh air in the garden until it was time to dress for dinner.

Chapter Six

That afternoon, after the girls had rested, Belinda was on her way to the schoolroom when she heard muffled sobbing. Going into the room Kitty and Sarah shared, she found Kitty with her head buried in her pillow crying bitterly, her eyes red, her cheeks puffy.

Belinda sat down and put her arm round her charge, lifting her head from the pillow. "Kitty dear, whatever is the matter?"

Kitty threw herself back onto the pillow again and muttered something indistinguishable.

"I did not hear a word of that," Belinda said bracingly. "I cannot possibly help you if you won't tell me clearly what the trouble is. Now," she fetched a face cloth wrung out in cold water from the washstand. "wipe your face with this while I find you a handkerchief." She produced one from Kitty's dresser.

Kitty obediently washed her face, dried it and blew her nose. She was still sniffing and taking little gasping breaths, but she was able to look Belinda in the eye.

"Where is Sarah?" Belinda wondered why Sarah had not come to tell her that her sister was distressed. Sarah loved minding other people's business.

"She has gone to play ball with Simon," said Kitty in a voice of tragedy.

"Why didn't you go too?"

This innocent question brought about a fresh storm of weeping and it was a little while before Belinda could restore Kitty's calm.

"That's just it: Simon didn't want me; he only wanted Sarah. All my brothers like her better than me. They're all being beastly to me." Kitty's eyes began to fill with tears of self-pity again.

"Surely not," said Belinda.

"Simon says I'm too old for ball games and won't let me play. Will said I behaved like a hoyden when he had his fight with Tom; he said he expected me to be more grown up. Will and I used to be such friends, Miss Farrington. We used to go into the fields and woods together but now he expects me to stay at home sewing and being lady-like." This thought almost caused Kitty to choke. "Then Clive gave me a horrid lecture—you know how awful his set-downs are. He said I behaved shockingly when we went to Blythburgh. He said such a rag-mannered girl as I would never have a beau unless I learned a little conduct."

"And Mr. Mark, has he said anything?"

"Mark doesn't care about me at all; he's only interested in females he can flirt with."

Belinda thought this unjust but did not comment on this subject. "Well, Kitty, you are nearly sixteen. You should be throwing off your childish ways and beginning to behave like a grown up lady with manners to match."

"I knew you'd say that," said Kitty resentfully, "because it's your job to turn me into a lady. But I feel no different now from when I was Sarah's age: I want to do all the things she does and enjoy myself."

"Sarah is only twelve—there's a deal of difference between you. It won't be long before we shall all be thinking about your come-out."

"Huh," said Kitty ungraciously, "you would never know it. I'm treated the same as her, I have to do the same lessons, go to bed at the same time as she does. We even have the same kind of dresses, hers in one colour and mine in another. How can I feel different if I'm not treated differently? Anyway, Sarah has always been the boys' favourite because she is the baby."

"I do see your point, Kitty, and I shall speak to your

mamma about your having some extra privileges and some more grown-up clothes now you are so nearly a woman. But you know, my dear, privileges have to be earned. You must make a greater effort."

Kitty was pleased by Belinda's promise but she still wasn't reconciled to her lot nor to Belinda's lecture.

"I don't see how you can possibly understand," she said resentfully. "You had no brothers so you cannot know how I feel about them preferring Sarah to me."

"But I don't think they do. They see you developing a woman's body and expect you have conduct to match it. It's true I was an only child, but I'm learning by observation what it means to be one of a family. I can see that you are much luckier than I was. True, my parents treated me as a treasured child, but I missed all the fun you Sheldons have together. Remember, Kitty, I had no-one young to talk to, no-one to play with, no-one with whom to share a joke or a secret. Always my companions were older people which is why you probably find me stuffy. I wish I had had brothers and sisters."

Belinda stopped. If she went on, she could easily slip into self-pity which would help neither her nor Kitty.

"Now," she said in a determinedly cheerful voice, "why not come and practise that sonata we have been studying and when it is ready, you can surprise your family with a dazzling display on the piano."

Kitty giggled weakly at the thought of dazzling them. Both she and Belinda knew her playing was no more than adequate but she fell in with Belinda's plan and dried her eyes.

Later that day, Belinda had a little talk with Mrs. Sheldon about Kitty's problems.

"I see what you mean, Miss Farrington. She is at a very difficult age: a child one moment and a woman grown the next. We must think up some extra treats for her. It has always been so easy to consider the two girls together, one forgets how different they are and that the gap between them is widening."

"Do you think, ma'am, that we could free the girls from their lessons until the boys go back to Westminster? I would, of course, still supervise their activities."

"That is a sensible plan, Miss Farrington. It must be difficult to keep them at their books. I should have thought of it but I have been worrying about those headstrong boys. They were always hey-go-mad, but school seems to have made them wilder than ever. But that's my problem, not yours. I must tell you I'm pleased with the way you are managing the girls."

Belinda glowed. She had begun to have doubts about her worth to Mrs. Sheldon. Although she was a selfish woman, she was kind when the kindness cost her nothing.

"You are looking a little peaky," she said to Belinda. "I see your bruise is fading, but I think you are still not quite yourself."

"I am well, thank you ma'am. My eye looks far worse than it feels." Belinda was still appalled every time she looked in the mirror and saw the discoloured flesh round her eye which was the greeny-yellowy colour of a stormy sky.

"I think you need some fresh air and a respite from this turbulent household. I know you are not used to having so many people round you all the time. Why not go for a ride, it is a beautiful afternoon. Ask them to saddle up Warrior. He carries a lady's saddle well."

"How kind you are, ma'am. A ride would be delightful, but what about the girls? Should I not take them too?"

"Mark always has time hanging heavy on his hands, I wonder he doesn't get into mischief. It will do him good to devise something to amuse his brothers and sisters. Go and enjoy yourself."

Belinda needed no more urging. She changed into her riding habit and went to the stables. Warrior was an elderly grey gelding and not as fierce as his name suggested. Ben tacked him up and put on a side saddle and helped her mount. He offered to accompany her but Belinda wanted to be on her own. She chose the coast road so that she could enjoy a gallop on the sands if the tide was out.

As she cantered along the grass above the dunes she heard moaning. Remembering the dog she and Clive had rescued a fortnight ago she feared it might be another trapped animal. Slowing Warrior to a walk, she went down onto the sand and threaded her way between the dunes, looking about her.

At first she couldn't see where the sound had come from or what had made it. She guided Warrior between the sandy hillocks, looking left and right. After a while, she caught a glimpse of light blue behind a dune and made towards it. She was surprised to find a man in a sky-blue uniform lying face down, motionless. His black three cornered hat was lying near and his sandy hair was matted with congealing blood.

It was Yardley, the riding officer. She jumped down, went over and tried to rouse him. "Mr. Yardley, what has happened?"

He groaned and lifted an ashen face. He tried to push himself up but slumped back onto the sand.

Belinda ran to a rock pool, dipped her pocket handkerchief in water, helped him turn over and bathed his face.

"Miss Farrington," he croaked, "you are an angel of mercy! Oh, my head—it aches abominably."

She was relieved to hear him speak. "I'm not surprised, you have a nasty wound; did you fall?"

"No," he said ruefully, "I was attacked. I found a cache of spirit kegs buried in the sand and began to dig. While I was intent upon my work, I felt a sharp crack on my head and then everything went black."

"The smugglers! Did you see them?"

"Alas no."

"When did this happen? How long have you been lying here?"

Yardley looked about him measuring the advance of the sea and the position of the sun. This seemed to hurt his eyes and he closed them quickly.

"About two hours ago, at a guess. Thank goodness you came to my aid. Otherwise I would have drowned when the tide came in."

Belinda thought this over-dramatic. "Nonsense. As soon as the water washed over you, you would have roused up."

He began to shake his head but stopped, wincing with pain. "Now I can believe you are a governess—are you so brisk with your charges?"

Belinda ignored this. "Where is your horse?"

"If the smugglers haven't taken him, he's tied to a gate nearby."

"Do you think you can walk if I help you? You can lean on Warrior."

Yardley stood up and tottering unsteadily, he began to walk, glad to use Warrior as a crutch. When they came to the gate, the black horse was waiting.

"How foolish of you to think the smugglers would have taken him: horse stealing is a capital offence," Belinda said.

"Do you still not believe in their wickedness?" he said bitterly, "Do you still refuse to help me catch them, even after you have seen the dastardly way they have treated me?"

Belinda stepped back. "Really, Mr. Yardley, you ask too much. Catching smugglers is no task for a woman. I have asked you not to speak of this to me."

"Do you still maintain no-one at Park Place is involved?" His pale blue eyes seemed to bore into her.

Belinda looked back steadily. Whatever misgivings she had, she was not prepared to share them with Frank Yardley. She could not like him; there was something about him that made her uneasy.

"Quite sure," she said firmly.

He cupped his hands and helped her remount Warrior.

"Do me one favour, if you please. Don't mention to anyone that you found me wounded on the sands. My credit here is low enough already."

Belinda promised, then turned Warrior towards the beach.

"I hope you will soon feel better, Mr. Yardley," she said, and put Warrior into a canter, then increased his speed to a gallop.

Belatedly Yardley remembered his manners. "Thank you," came faintly to her as she raced across the sands.

The sensation of speed exhilarated her and all her worries blew away. When at last she turned Warrior's head for home and retraced her steps at a sober pace she thought about Yardley. He was so obsessed with smugglers that he saw them everywhere. She wondered if he had really been hit on the head or if he had fallen catching his head on a rock and had made up the story to cover his discomfiture. Perhaps that was unfair, but he irritated her and she could not think well of him.

Whoever the Master-smuggler was, Belinda was sure he was more than a match for Yardley.

* * *

Two days later, Belinda decided to go into Woodbridge to do some shopping.

"You shall come with me," she said to Kitty and Sarah. "Go and change while I see if your mamma has any commissions for us."

Mrs. Sheldon wanted Belinda to enquire of the clock maker whether her carriage clock had yet been repaired. Will and Simon, hearing of the projected trip, begged to be included.

It was another brilliant June day so they had the hood of the barouche down. Belinda and Will sat facing the front with Kitty and Sarah opposite. Simon elected to sit on the box beside the coachman rather than squash inside. Richard, the footman, completed the entourage, standing, wooden faced on the step at the back.

Kitty and Sarah wore similar carriage dresses of green and

blue spotted cambric with high crowned bonnets trimmed
with matching flowers. Belinda's lavender dress was trimmed
with a deep flounce of violet silk. A dashing jockey bonnet of
alternating lavender and violet stripes tied with a rakish bow
under her ear sat becomingly on her dark curls.

Will, seeing how fine his sisters and their governess looked,
apologised for his old green coat and shabby boots. He
explained he had been fishing when he heard of the
expedition and had not had time to change. He was not even
wearing a cravat—his shirt was open at the neck like a poet's.
Simon was his usual grubby, urchin-like self. He quickly
became absorbed in conversation with Foster about horses.

At Woodbridge, Foster drove into the yard of The Crown
to bait the horses and wait while they did their shopping.
Will wanted to go down to the harbour to see Old Valentine
and arrange for some fishing later in the week and Simon
chose to go with him. Sarah looked wistfully after them, but
before she could beg to join them, Belinda swept her off to
the shops on Market Hill. She instructed the boys to return
within the hour.

After Belinda had visited the clock maker, she went to the
apothecary for some tooth-powder and violet soap, then she
led the girls to the haberdashers. She sat on a chair and asked
the obsequious young shopman to show her stockings, both
silk and cotton thread. He bowed, fetched a pile of paste-
board boxes, began to open them and display the hosiery.

Sarah sighed; she was bored and fidgety, running her
fingers along the edge of the mahogany counter.

"Pray don't," said Belinda. "You will dirty your gloves. Try
to keep still. As soon as I have selected some stockings, we can
go."

At that moment the shop door crashed back on its hinges
and Simon burst in, red-faced and panting. He grabbed
Belinda's arm and shook it.

"Come quickly, Miss Farrington. The pressgang is by the
harbour and they've taken up Will!"

Belinda started to her feet, stockings forgotten, and made for the door. She hurried down the street looking agitated, closely followed by Kitty and Sarah. Simon explained as they went. "We were down by the harbour talking to Old Valentine when we heard a commotion. The pressgang was taking fishermen—and taking them pretty roughly too. They carry cudgels, you know, and they don't hesitate to hit fellows over the head if they resist.

"There goo poor young Barty," Old Valentine said and then, before we could say a word, the petty officer grabbed Will.

"Yo ho, brother," he said. "You look a strong lad: bred to the sea, I'll warrant. Just what King George's navy needs."

"Will didn't argue or put up any resistance. He grinned at me, shrugged and went off with them. I piked it back to you as quick as I could."

"Poor Will," Sarah moaned.

"What will you do, Miss Farrington?" Kitty asked.

"I shall remonstrate with them," said Belinda bravely, but her heart was beating fast.

As they hurried down the hill, they saw coming towards them the riding officer. Belinda greeted him with relief.

"Mr. Yardley, how thankful I am to meet you. Please will you help me? Young Will Sheldon has been taken up by the pressgang and I must get him released. Could you use your influence in his behalf?"

Yardley touched his hat in salute and looked stern. "I fear you will have little success, Miss Farrington."

"Won't you even try to help us?" Belinda said indignantly.

"It would do no good. Perhaps if you were to see a magistrate..."

Belinda was furious. "There's no time for that." She pushed past him. "It's lucky for you I didn't refuse to help you when you needed assistance two days ago. Come, Simon, we must get there before they start taking their captives aboard ship." Belinda was almost running now, the children trotting beside her. At last they came to the waterside.

When Belinda saw the pressgang, her spirits quailed. Men detailed for pressgang duty were the burliest sailors in the crew, chosen for their size to impress and intimidate. They wore varnished hats, blue canvas jackets and wide-legged trousers; their pigtails were tarred and bound with canvas strips. They carried cutlasses and cudgels to add to their air of menace. Belinda wrinkled her nose. The smell of salt, tar, and sweat was overpowering.

In the centre of the gang were their prisoners, hands tied behind their backs, some looking dazed, some looking frightened. Will was among them, looking more interested than scared.

Belinda went straight up to the beefy petty officer who was in charge.

"Sir," she said breathlessly, "there has been a terrible mistake. That young man," pointing at Will, "should not have been taken. He is a gentleman's son and therefore exempt from pressing." She knew that this was the law.

"Ho yus," said the man, running insolent eyes over her in a way she did not like, "and Hi am the Emperor of China."

"Don't be impertinent!" Belinda drew herself up to her full five feet two inches, but still looked like David defying Goliath. "I say again, he is exempt. Release him at once!"

The man grinned. "Now look, Missy, anyone can see from his shabby clothes he ain't a gent and he came willing. It was a nice try but it won't fadge. You're his sweetheart, I suppose. Say good-bye, dearie, for you won't see him for many a long day. We'll have him blockading Boulogne before you can say 'God Save the King'."

Simon pushed himself forward. "If you're taking my brother, take me too!"

"Simon," cried Belinda grabbing the collar of his coat, "Have a care what you say."

The petty officer was tickled by this. "Grow a bit, sonny, and we'll take you next time round."

"Couldn't I be a powder monkey?" Simon asked wistfully.

The sailors were laughing as Belinda dragged Simon away. "Don't despair, Will," she called over her shoulder. "Your father will get you out." She gave Simon a shake. "Run back to The Crown and tell Foster to put the horses to. We must return to Park Place as soon as we can."

Sarah was almost in tears as they climbed the hill, but Kitty was indignant.

"Can you believe that odious riding officer? He might have tried to help."

Belinda was equally angry. Yardley must have known as well as she did that Will was exempt and his word added to hers would have freed him. And what ingratitude after the help she had given him! His dislike of the Sheldons must be even stronger than she had thought.

"If only Will had been wearing his smart London clothes, this would never have happened," Kitty said mournfully.

They scrambled into the barouche which Foster had ready. He needed no urging to spring his horses, Simon having told him what had happened. The barouche swayed as they sped along the hot, dusty lanes.

"Ventre à terre, the way they go in novels," said Sarah happily as they bucketed along. The excitement and the speed seemed to have restored her spirits.

Suddenly the pace slowed as Foster reined in.

"Why are you slowing down?" Belinda called.

"It's Mr. Clive a'coming, Miss."

The tall, unmistakable figure came towards them, elegantly dressed as always, mounted on Soldier, his spirited bay.

"Thank God!" said Belinda, her hands clasped together. She looked up at Clive trustingly as he stopped beside the barouche.

"What is wrong, Miss Farrington?"

"Oh Clive! I was never so happy to see anyone in my life!" She was so agitated that she didn't notice she had committed the solecism of addressing him by his Christian name.

Clive didn't seem to mind. He smiled and patted her hand reassuringly as he listened to the story. He soothed Belinda's agitation and sent the barouche on its way while he rode into Woodbridge to rescue his brother.

All the way home, Belinda worried about giving Mrs. Sheldon the news, expecting strong hysterics—but she was wrong. Mrs. Sheldon said calmly, "How tiresome! Don't worry Miss Farrington. I have every confidence in Clive's ability to bring Will home safely."

Belinda was surprised but relieved. She took the girls and Simon up to the schoolroom and suggested a game to occupy them.

Kitty put on an air of tragedy. "How can you think of Speculation while poor Will is suffering in the hold of a nasty ship."

"What fustian!" Simon scoffed. "It'd be capital fun to be a sailor."

"It would be horrid," Sarah said with a shudder. "I've heard they have rotting food and live so close together there is hardly room to turn round."

"And there's the lash," said Belinda then seeing the horrified faces of Kitty and Sarah, wished she hadn't mentioned it.

Simon laughed harshly. "Lord, you might be describing school. I wish the pressgang had taken me too: it'd be a sight more interesting learning about navigation than those deadly Latin verbs they stuff us with. As for the lash—naval floggings can't be much worse than the Bagwig's birchings. I really fancy life on the ocean wave."

Belinda was startled. "But Simon, if you really want to go to sea there's no need of the pressgang, you could go as an officer as your rank entitles you to do."

Kitty had one of those lightning changes of mood that so astonished Belinda.

"Like brave Lord Nelson," she cried, eyes shining. "He was my hero! Wouldn't Will make a splendid admiral?"

"Simon would too," said Sarah loyally.

Belinda hid a smile. "Pressed men are hardly likely to rise to such heights but we are worrying unnecessarily, Mr. Clive will bring Will off safely."

The girls were less sanguine but Belinda was proved right. The gong had rung for dinner and they were just going into the dining room when Clive, looking unruffled and Will, looking sulky, arrived.

Mrs. Sheldon sent them to wash but said they need not change their dress on this occasion.

During the meal, Will was bombarded with questions. He explained how he had been taken, but to everyone's astonishment, he was furious that Clive had rescued him.

"I was glad when they took me," he said resentfully, "I'd far rather go to sea than back to school. I was thinking what a prime lark it was when Clive rode up and spoiled everything. He told the man in charge I was a gentleman's son and his brother; he greased him in the fist and I was let go." He glowered at his brother. "Why did you interfere?"

"Ungrateful puppy!" growled Mr. Sheldon. "Fine thing if Clive had left you there."

"Well it would have been," Will retorted hotly, "I would have liked it."

"I thought you had your heart set on the army, that you wanted Papa to buy you a pair of colours," Mark said.

"Changed my mind," Will said sulkily, "I prefer the navy to the army and I'd have been in the navy if Clive hadn't stuck his oar in."

"Oars—boats—the navy!" chortled Mark. "Very good, Will."

"You can boil your head," Will said crossly.

"Ingrate!" Mr. Sheldon said angrily. "Say no more, the subject's closed. Pass the buttered crabs."

Later, when the ladies retired to the drawing room while the gentlemen took port, Mrs. Sheldon said,

"Kitty go over to the pianoforte and choose some music.

You shall play when the gentlemen join us and Sarah can turn the pages for you."

As the girls drifted over to the piano, she moved closer to Belinda and said in a low voice, "I haven't thanked you yet, Miss Farrington, for the efforts you made in Will's behalf. It was very good of you. It is really not the part of a governess to concern herself with the boys in a family, only to care for the girls in her charge."

"But I wasn't successful, ma'am, there's nothing to thank me for. I am ashamed that I didn't manage to get him released."

"You must realise that females carry little weight in this world, Miss Farrington. Do not reproach yourself: you did your best." She sighed deeply. "I don't know what's come over Will! I cannot like this barring out, this revolutionary talk, this eagerness to become a common seaman."

"Simon spoke the same way earlier about wishing to go to sea. Do not take this suggestion amiss, ma'am, but might not the navy be the answer for them? I don't mean the pressgang, of course, but could they not enter the service as midshipmen? My papa was used to say that a naval education was equal to that gained at a public school and the discipline was stronger. I beg your pardon if you think my suggestion encroaching."

Mrs. Sheldon stared at Belinda who blushed. "I'm sorry ma'am, I've said too much. I shouldn't have spoken."

"But I'm glad you did, Miss Farrington, I wonder I didn't think of it myself. I've been worrying what to do about those boys: I think the navy might be just the thing. They can always sell out after the war if the life doesn't suit."

When Mr. Sheldon and his sons joined the ladies, Mrs. Sheldon took her husband aside and begged a few words with him in his book room. As they left she said, "Now, Kitty, I want you to play nicely for your brothers. Miss Farrington, please see that she does."

"I hope she won't sing," said Simon gloomily, "I'd rather

listen to moggies caterwauling."

"Simon!" said Belinda, "how unkind."

"That'll do, Scamp," said Mark shaking him by the collar. "I'll keep him in order, Miss Farrington."

She smiled gratefully.

As Kitty began to play, Clive came and sat down by Belinda's side.

"Do you know what Mamma is up to? I thought I saw the gleam of battle in her eyes."

Belinda said diffidently, "I think it is an idea I mentioned." She looked down at her lap, feeling awkward about her faux pas at their last meeting. "You see, Mr. Clive..."

"I prefer it when you drop the 'Mister'," he said gravely, although his eyes were twinkling.

"Don't roast me, sir, I did not mean to be so unbecomingly familiar."

"But I liked it, especially if I may call you Belinda." He smiled in a way that made Belinda feel giddy. "Tell me what you said to Mamma."

"I suggested that as the boys seem so keen on the navy, they might perhaps go to sea as midshipmen. I understand the education is excellent."

Clive looked startled.

"I see you think I was presumptuous," Belinda said miserably.

"No, I was merely surprised, I realise you have their welfare in mind. Did Mamma not shudder at the thought of her darlings going into action?"

"She did not say so. She thought it an excellent scheme."

Clive spoke thoughtfully. "Running up and down the rigging would hold no terrors for them, they are used to the rough and tumble of school, and naval discipline would be the making of them. Midshipmen usually enter the service at twelve, but I am sure Papa will know a Captain who would take them at this late stage. The more I think about it the more I like it." He turned to Mark.

"What do you think of the idea? Miss Farrington has suggested to Mamma that the harum-scarum boys should go to sea as midshipmen."

Simon heard this. "What?" he said, "How famous! Oh Miss Farrington, you are a trump! Will she let us?"

A plaintive voice from the piano said, "May I stop playing as no-one is listening?"

"Yes do stop," Mark said. "Our ears have been punished enough."

Kitty stuck her tongue out at her brother. Belinda reproved her but frowned at Mark.

"Don't tease, sir. You played very nicely, Kitty."

Kitty and Sarah came over and joined their brothers.

"What's going on, Will?" Sarah asked.

Will, looking more cheerful than he had all evening, explained.

Sarah gasped and rounded on Belinda. "How could you, Miss Farrington! You want the boys sent away to make your life easier. If Will and Simon go to sea because of your words, I'll never forgive you and I'll never, ever do anything you tell me to again!"

"Don't be so gothic, Bratling," said Will giving her arm a little shake, "You're not to pull caps with Miss Farrington over us; we want to go."

Mrs. Sheldon came into the room. "Will, Simon, go to your Papa. I think you will like to hear what he has to say."

Joyfully, the boys leaped to their feet and ran from the room playfully punching each other's arms.

Sarah, her face contorted with anger, hurled a cushion at Belinda, burst into tears and ran out after them.

Chapter Seven

Belinda was dismayed at the magnitude of the rift between herself and the two girls caused by her suggestion that Will and Simon should go to sea.

The rest of the family praised Belinda for her finding a solution to their problem; Mr. and Mrs. Sheldon and Clive were sure the discipline would be the making of the boys. Mark was happy they were doing something they wanted: it made him all the more impatient to be off to India: his ship didn't sail until September and he felt the clock was moving with leaden hands. The harum-scarum boys were ecstatic but Sarah was not to be consoled and Kitty followed her lead.

Mrs. Sheldon was in a permanent flutter in the days that followed, buying clothes and packing sea chests. Mr. Sheldon conferred with friends in high places and was soon able to announce berths had been secured for his younger sons with a post captain of his acquaintance. Will and Simon crowed like dung-hill cocks.

Kitty and Sarah continued to be angry, constantly blaming Belinda. They made her life as difficult as possible. There were no more pleasant sewing sessions while Belinda read to them: they told her they did not wish to hear The Orphan of the Rhine—it was dreary stuff, not a patch on their old favourite, Sir Charles Grandison. Their water colours were spoiled by spilt paint water. The shell boxes they were making were mysteriously marred. Sarah's handwriting looked like the inky tracks of a drunken spider and her stitches were larger than ever. When French conversation was required they vowed they could not understand a word Belinda said. Even riding became a penance: Sarah set off at a gallop and claimed her mount had bolted while Kitty lagged behind declaring her pony a sluggard.

Mrs. Sheldon saw what was happening but did not interfere thinking Belinda would do better if she could work things out herself. But she pitied her and occasionally gave her a respite from the girls' childish behaviour by sending her on an errand. The hot weather had ripened the grapes in her conservatory so one afternoon she sent her over with Will to deliver some of her muscatels to the Hallingburys.

Belinda knew what was behind the errand and was grateful. As Will drove the gig inland through the woods to Tunstall, she found the shade of the tall trees a relief from the glaring July sun, and Will's cheerful, friendly presence was a balm after the sulks of his sisters. Now he had dropped all pretensions to dandyism. His languid air had gone and he was an amusing companion.

"Why Mamma wants to favour Mrs. Hallingbury, I cannot think," he confided. "She's a sour old thing and as for Isabella, I've seldom known a more tiresome female. We're in for a dreary afternoon."

Belinda laughed. "I expect we are. I shall be ignored. Miss Hallingbury doesn't care for lowly people like governesses."

"What stuff," said Will. "That shows what a stupid girl she is. Thank goodness Clive is not so taken with her nowadays. At one time we feared they might make a match of it. We all dreaded the thought of having her for a sister."

Belinda would have liked to ask more about this but at that moment a small dark man ran out of the wood and called to them.

"Monsieur, mademoiselle: aide moi, je vous en prie!"

Will pulled up. "What's the fellow saying?"

"Surely your French is up to that, Will?"

"Don't understand a word," he said. "They don't teach us useful things like French and Spanish at school. Only dead languages like Latin and Greek."

"He's asking us to help him." She spoke to the man in French. "What's the matter? How can we help you?"

In rapid French with many gestures, the man explained that he had come over with a contraband cargo the previous night. While helping with the unloading he had become separated from his compatriots and had been left behind. He spoke no English and did not know how to contact anyone in the organisation. Could they put him in touch with the smugglers so he could return to France from the next rendezvous?

Belinda relayed all this to Will.

"Hmm," Will said, "sounds fishy to me. How do we know he's not an exciseman in disguise? Yardley would give his eye-teeth to learn how to contact the smugglers."

"I don't think he's one of Yardley's men. He speaks idiomatically and he looks French."

"That's all very well but we're at war with the Frogs—he might be a spy. We ought to hand him over to a constable or a magistrate."

The little dark man was anxiously looking from one to the other following the exchange without comprehending.

"The young gentleman thinks you might be in the pay of the excisemen," Belinda told him.

The Frenchman's eyes flashed: he spat and swore.

Belinda turned pink. "Not Yardley's man," she said to Will, then she asked the man, "Are you spying for l'Empereur?"

The little man made a long speech with many gestures.

"What's he prosing on about?" Will enquired.

"He says he's a peasant, a fisherman: he thinks nothing of politics. He only wants to earn enough to make his family comfortable."

Will nodded. "That's what one of our fellows would say. If you think he's genuine, then I vote we help him."

"But how?"

Will frowned. "We ought to go to the top man in the organisation. I know most of the servants and estate workers are in the smugglers' pay, but they won't know the Master-smuggler's name and I don't know who it is."

"Should we ask your brothers? They may know." Belinda's stomach fluttered. Was she at last going to find out who the Master-smuggler was?

"No good asking Clive; he wouldn't know, he's too starched up—always prosing on about right and wrong. Mark's up to all the rigs and rows, he might know who it is. We'll take this fellow back to Park Place and hide him in the summerhouse. While you speak to Mark, I'll turn Cookie up sweet and get him some food." He grinned wickedly. "He can start on these grapes."

He made signs to the man to get into the gig and lie on the floor. Belinda covered him with a rug and handed him the basket of grapes which the man fell upon wolfishly.

"What will you tell your mother?" she asked.

Will grinned. "I shall say the grapes were received rapturously and eaten with great enjoyment."

Belinda giggled.

* * *

The grounds of Park Place were surrounded by a wall. Will stopped the gig beside it and told Belinda to hold the reins while he took the man and hid him in the summerhouse. Belinda explained to the Frenchman what was happening and with many thanks to Belinda, he followed Will over the wall.

When Will returned, he said, "Go and find Mark while I sweet-talk Cookie. I'll meet you in the schoolroom later."

While Will went to the kitchen, Belinda went to find Mark. He was reading the London newspapers that had come down on the Ipswich mail. Although they were several days old they were still full of interest, but he willingly put them aside to listen to her story.

"Why come to me? What makes you think I know who the Master-smuggler is?"

"Will and I thought you'd be more sympathetic than Mr.

Clive. Have you no notion to whom we should take the man?"

Mark chuckled. "Clive would be sure to pull a long face. But Miss Farrington, you and Will are playing with fire: how do you know the man's not a spy or Yardley's pawn?"

"I really don't think he is. His language and his bearing convinced me." She told him what the man had said about the excise service and about politics.

"Perhaps you're right, but you'd do better not to meddle. If you're determined to get involved, go and see Jem the blacksmith."

"Jem? Is he the Master-smuggler?"

"No, silly girl, I told you, it has to be someone with money and brains; but Jem's in it—he's the strong-arm man who keeps the rabble in order. Take Warrior out and pretend he's cast a shoe. That will be reason enough to stop at the smithy."

Belinda hurried off to change into her riding habit. Mrs. Sheldon had given her permission to ride Warrior whenever she was free.

She rode to the village and at the smithy, she felt foolish pretending to have cast a shoe but she whispered her tale to Jem while he was examining Warrior's hooves. Jem looked at her with a piercing blue stare which made Belinda feel quite nervous.

"In the summerhouse, is he? You leave it with me, Missy. I'll deal with the Frenchy. Now don't you goo a'sayin' nothin' to no-one about it."

Belinda shook her head and accepted Jem's help to remount. As she rode back to Park Place, her feelings were strangely mixed. She was glad she had helped the man, but she felt guilty at having done so. Now she was as culpable as any smuggler. Although she had acted out of charity to a fellow human being, she still felt blame-worthy. She was frightened of Jem who was menacing as well as big and powerful. Cravenly she thought she would rather be on the wrong side of Yardley than Jem.

* * *

Often in the days that followed she wondered if the man had got home safely but there was no-one she could ask—certainly not Jem—she was beginning to realise that the less one knew about the activities of the Gentlemen, the better. Neither Mark nor Will referred to the matter again so there was no way of knowing.

At the end of July the day came for Will and Simon's departure. They came up to the schoolroom dressed in their new uniforms to show themselves off and say good-bye.

Kitty and Sarah were in floods of tears when the boys left and Belinda, knowing that they blamed her, did not attempt to pacify them. She left them wallowing in misery and took herself off for a walk round the lake. Under the shade of the willow trees she came upon Mark fishing. He gave her a welcoming smile and seemed pleased to see her.

"All alone, Miss Farrington? Where are the ghastly girls today?" he asked with a smile.

"You ought not to speak so about your sisters, sir." Belinda couldn't help smiling back. "They are in the schoolroom, crying bitterly, mourning the departure of the midshipmen."

"What stuff! Why should they be any unhappier to have the boys away at sea than away at school? Granted they might be away longer but on the other hand, they'll get leave whenever their ship is in port."

"Perhaps they fear the dangers of war for them."

"The girls may tremble but the harum-scarum boys won't regard that. Anyway, they'll probably never see a battle but will spend their time sailing up and down the Channel keeping the Frogs in harbour.

"Now if they were to cry for me," he said throwing out his line, "I could see the sense of it. When I go off to India next month, they won't see me again for years. But there, they probably won't miss me at all."

Belinda watched with distaste as he secured a wriggling worm to his hook.

"I'm sure they will, we'll all miss you," she said politely.

He moved along the bank and came closer to her. "You too, Belinda?" he said lightly.

Her heart skipped a beat at this familiarity but she decided to ignore it.

"Are you looking forward to going?"

"Indeed I am. There's not enough to do here to keep me out of mischief. Papa has told me wonderful tales of what my life will be serving the East India Company and I shall come home rich as Croesus." He cast his line again and moved nearer. "Have you ever thought of going abroad?"

She shook her head.

"Why don't you come with me? Papa says India is beautiful, wild and untamed, full of colour and mystery. You'd live like a princess, waited on hand and foot with no hoydens to civilise—think of that! You would be a lady of leisure and I could afford to buy you beautiful clothes and jewels: say yes and come with me."

Was this an honourable proposal? Belinda looked up at his smiling face, trying to discern whether he was serious or teasing. If it were the latter and she gave a serious answer, he would laugh and she would feel foolish. Instead she spoke lightly.

"The last thing you need in your baggage is a penniless governess—you will find many lovely young Englishwomen there and with your good looks and address will be able to take your pick."

"Perhaps you are right." Mark sighed, drew in his line and laid his fishing rod down. "But you're devilish attractive, Belinda. I've been longing to kiss your rosy lips ever since I first saw you that first day when you stepped off the coach."

Belinda blushed, took a step back and found she could move no further, her back against a tree. "What nonsense, sir. If you are going to say such things, I shall return to the house."

Mark jumped forward and took her in his arms. He pressed a passionate kiss onto her mouth that took her breath away. The kiss was insistent and went on far too long for Belinda's comfort.

"Oh Belinda! You tantalising little morsel." Mark's face was flushed. He turned and picked up his fishing rod again and busied himself with the hook. "Think about what I've said, my dear: it may be the best offer you'll ever have."

Belinda turned away and hurried back to the house. She was agitated and uncertain still of his intentions but surely, after such a kiss he must be serious. If indeed he was, it was not what she wanted. She liked Mark but his passionate kiss had not stirred her as much as the light touch of Clive's hand had done. However, the kiss had told her something: it had shown that there was only one man for her and it was not Mark. She was aware that Mark felt free to kiss her without their coming to an understanding because she was a mere governess and that for the same reason, Clive would never do so.

Her heart was aching. It was Clive that she loved even though she feared he might be the Master-smuggler, but even if he were not, the case was hopeless: Clive was above her touch and would never show her more than kindness and courtesy.

* * *

The day after the boys left, Mrs. Sheldon called Clive into her boudoir.

"I'm worried about Miss Farrington," she said. "The girls are treating her abominably. She's very patient and I do not want to interfere and destroy her authority but I feel like boxing their ears. As usual, Sarah is the ring-leader and Kitty follows her lead."

"Sarah will soon forget her anger," he said soothingly.

Mrs. Sheldon was not comforted. "I don't want Miss Farrington to resign: she's the best governess we've ever had, well-informed and well-connected."

"Too good for such a position," agreed Clive.

"She wouldn't have taken it if she hadn't lost her parents and her fiancé."

Clive frowned. "Her fiancé? I had no idea she had been engaged."

"Yes, I understand he was a Lieutenant in the Rifle Brigade. He lost his life in a skirmish in the Peninsula—Talavera or some such outlandish place, I think it was."

Clive felt a stab of jealousy for the man Belinda had cared for enough to promise to marry him.

Mrs. Sheldon went on. "She could move in the best circles did she wish to do so: she was offered a London season as Lady Anselm's protégée or she might have gone to live with her uncle at Farlow Hall, but she was determined to be independent which is unusual in one so young."

"But admirable," said Clive thoughtfully. "She's a pluck to the backbone. I'll try to think of something to take the girls' minds off their loss, but I think they'll settle down now the boys have sailed." He kissed his mother good-bye.

As he rode over to one of the outlying farms on the estate that morning, Belinda was much in his mind. His opinion of her had changed greatly since her arrival three months previously. His initial impression had been of a small, neat young woman with a lovely face, candid grey eyes and an air of distinction but he had thought her unsuitable as a governess and far too young to control his sisters. He had decided she was a trifle giddy after her escapades on the ladder outside his room and up the tree rescuing the kitten. He had dismissed her as goosish and had said some scalding things to her but he couldn't help liking her: she had not been cowed by his criticism.

As the days wore on, he decided she was far from goosish

but had solid worth. She had shown Isabella up for the shallow creature she was by her fearless rescue of the dog; she had shown courage trying to disentangle Will from the pressgang and when she tried to stop Will's fight with Tom.

He hoped his mother was wrong and that his sisters' tiresome behaviour would not cause her to resign. He wouldn't like that at all, the house without her presence would no longer be as pleasant to live in.

By a lucky chance, he found the very thing to heal the breach between Belinda and his sisters in Farmer Prosser's stable. In one of the loose boxes he saw a litter of unusual-looking puppies. Bess, their mother, was a sheepdog but the puppies didn't look like collies, they had tight black curls, pendulous ears and rounder features.

"What have you been up to, Bess to produce such a strange looking litter?" Clive asked with mock severity. "Who is the sire, Prosser?"

Prosser said he suspected the large poodle up at the Hall.

"I don't know what I'm a'goin' to do with them, sir: they won't be no good for sheep and I doubt they'll train up for the gun and seemingly, they'll be too gentle for guard dogs. Bess is that fond of them that I haven't the heart to put them down."

Clive was fondling an importunate puppy that had taken a fancy to the toe of his boot and was worrying it with needle teeth and trying to growl. He grinned.

"I'll take this one off your hands, Prosser. I think my sisters would like him as a pet."

Much to Prosser's satisfaction, a coin changed hands and when Clive had finished his business, he took the perky puppy up on his saddle bow.

"You'll have to learn manners, young dog," he said severely and then laughed at the adoring look in the little creature's eyes. He grimaced as it licked his hand.

"Don't try to make love to me, sir! That won't pay toll. Let's hope you get a warm welcome in the schoolroom."

He need not have worried about the puppy's reception. The furry bundle was received with rapture.

"Clive, is he indeed for us? How kind you are," said Sarah. In her excitement, she forgot her campaign against Belinda and appealed to her. "Isn't he the dearest little thing, Miss Farrington?"

Belinda agreed and smiled warmly at Clive, guessing his motive.

"The puppy must have a collar with his name and address engraved on a silver plate," said Kitty. "Will you have one made for him, Clive?"

"Certainly not! It would be useless to put more than a thong or shoe string on him until he has grown."

Belinda, conscious of her need to point lessons wherever she could said, "Prince Frederick had a dog whose collar tag read, 'I am His Highness' dog at Kew, Pray sir, whose dog are you?' Perhaps you could compose a couplet for your dog's collar."

"What a capital notion, Miss Farrington," said Clive with a sigh, although his eyes were alight with laughter. "I shall be surprised, though, if their rhyme matches Alexander Pope's. I see you mean me to dig deep in my pocket for this rascal."

Belinda blushed which made Kitty and Sarah giggle. A truce seemed to have been declared.

"You don't mind our having the puppy, do you. Miss Farrington?" Sarah said.

"Not in the least, but I make one rule: you girls must look after him yourselves, feed him, care for him and clear up after him when accidents happen—as they surely will."

"Of course we will. You're a brick, Miss Farrington," said Kitty with a happy grin.

Belinda was delighted. "I think we should bathe him before he takes up residence in the schoolroom, don't you agree, sir?"

Clive nodded. "He may well have picked up ticks or fleas on the farm."

As if to confirm this, the puppy started to scratch his ear vigorously with his hind leg.

"Out in the yard for you," Belinda said firmly. "Kitty, ask one of the stable boys to provide a tub, Sarah find aprons and towels. I'll bring the puppy down."

Kitty and Sarah ran to do Belinda's bidding, all thoughts of rebellion forgotten.

"What a splendid idea of yours," Belinda said to Clive. "I am so grateful."

"I hope it may prove to ease your burden rather than add to it, although I know from experience training puppies is hard work."

"Does Mrs. Sheldon approve?"

"She will, never fear. I shall go and tell her now and when the puppy is clean, the girls can show him to her." He went off to see his mother while Belinda took the squirming bundle down to the yard.

"The darling puppy must have a name," said Kitty, cuddling him while the bath was prepared. "What do you think of Bouncer?"

"I like it," said Belinda.

"Well I don't," said Sarah flatly. "That's a farm dog's name, he needs something grander."

The puppy was lowered into warm water. Kitty held him while Sarah rubbed his black curls with a bar of yellow soap.

"He has taken well to water—why not call him after a naval hero?" Belinda suggested.

"After my own special hero, Lord Nelson," cried Kitty. "Let's call him Horatio."

"That's far too long," argued Sarah.

Kitty made a face. "What if we shorten it to Horry?"

This was agreed upon. Belinda had nearly bitten her tongue when she heard herself saying 'naval hero' fearing she had called their attention to the departed midshipmen, but it seemed the boys took second place to the new acquisition. While the puppy was washed and rinsed, he was constantly informed his name was Horry.

"Wouldn't Will and Simon like him?" Kitty said wistfully. Belinda held her breath.

"I think it's as well they're not here," Sarah said, "you know what boys are, they might have teased dear little Horry."

Belinda opened her mouth and shut it again: the girls were completely unpredictable.

To begin with Horry was docile, but he soon began to tire of his bath and decided to look for a fresh adventure. With a sudden heave and a shake, he showered his attendants with water. Sarah and Kitty squeaked, let go of him and drew back. Horry, no longer restrained, made to leap from the tub. Belinda leaned forward to catch him but Horry's patience was at an end and he wriggled with great determination. Belinda lost her balance and as the dog escaped, she fell head first into the tub of soapy water.

She came up gasping, soap in her eyes, her dark hair flattened against her head. Kitty and Sarah went into shrieking paroxysms of laughter. At that moment Clive came round the corner to find his sisters convulsed, Belinda wet and angry and Horry pouncing at the edge of the tub barking hysterically.

Clive scooped him up disregarding the fact that the puppy was soaking his blue, superfine coat and his expensive silver and blue striped waistcoat.

"Hush, sir, be quiet! Kitty, Sarah, control yourselves." He tried to be stern but without success.

Belinda struggled to her feet gasping from her drenching and mortified that once again Clive had seen her lose her dignity and that the girls were laughing at her. She looked at Clive's face: he was smiling—no, he was grinning: a moment later he was laughing openly.

Her humiliation was complete. All the misery of the last few weeks when she had borne the girls' scorn without complaint welled up and she burst into tears.

"You are hateful—all of you! I'm going to pack! I won't stay here another minute."

Belinda fled from the yard, her cheeks scarlet.

Kitty and Sarah stopped laughing and looked at each other guiltily. Clive went white. Handing the puppy to Kitty, he said curtly,

"Dry the puppy and bring him up to the schoolroom. I don't know whether it can be done, but I will try to mend matters with Miss Farrington."

* * *

Belinda threw herself on the bed just as she was, wet and untidy and sobbed in a fit of self-pity. Her dignity was destroyed, Clive did not have any regard for her; if he had felt for her as she was beginning to hope he did, he would not have laughed at her predicament.

She would not put up with humiliation any longer: she would give notice, pack her boxes and return to Aunt Henshaw in Harrogate. After a short visit to recruit her strength, she would apply for a post as companion to a rich old lady. Elderly people might be crotchety but they could not possibly be as trying as this wild household.

Above her sobs, she heard a scratching at her door. Mark's voice said,

"Miss Farrington, I cannot bear to hear you crying, please let me talk to you."

Belinda sat up and looked around wildly. "You cannot come in here, sir—that would be most improper."

"No, no. I'll wait in the schoolroom; please dry your eyes and come and talk."

Belinda didn't want to speak to anyone. Since Mark had kissed her, she wasn't sure how to treat him, but at least he was kind and it was childish to sulk.

She changed her dress, towelled her hair briskly and splashed cold water on her red eyes. Her mirror told her she looked a fright but that could not be helped.

"I'm sorry my crying disturbed you," she said defensively when she entered the schoolroom.

Mark was beside her in a moment and put his arm round her shoulders.

"Poor Miss Farrington, it is for me to say I'm sorry that my brother and my sisters have distressed you."

Belinda sniffed back the tears this kind comment threatened to start. "It is foolish of me to allow them to upset me, but it is of no consequence. I have made up my mind to give your mamma my notice."

Mark's blue eyes were full of concern. "Please don't. You know what I think of you and Mamma values you highly. She says you are the best governess we have ever had. We need you to brighten our lives."

Belinda gave a tremulous smile. "I was not engaged to amuse you, sir."

"No but we cannot do without you." His blue eyes were smiling. "Clive thinks so too."

Belinda stiffened. "Mr. Clive," she said bitterly, "is utterly detestable and says the most odious things. He makes me more uncomfortable even than the girls."

It was unfortunate that it was at this moment that Clive came through the schoolroom door. His face was pale, his expression stiff.

"It is said that eavesdroppers seldom hear good of themselves. How true! I'd no idea I was so repellent. Don't worry, Miss Farrington, you may be assured I shall keep out of your way in future."

As he turned on his heel and ran down the stairs Belinda burst into another storm of weeping, this time so great that it was beyond Mark's powers to comfort her.

Chapter Eight

Belinda did not, after all, resign. When she was calmer she decided she must face up to her responsibilities—it would be chicken-hearted to run away. She had chosen to be a governess and must persevere. She must forget her feelings for Clive and concentrate on her work. She realised she had been an ineffective disciplinarian because she had tried to please her charges. She knew now that this was wrong: for a governess, respect was more important than liking. She was going to harden her heart and begin a rigorous programme of improvement.

When Kitty and Sarah apologised for their unkind laughter. Belinda brought herself to say, "It is of no consequence, I realise I must have looked comical. But now, young ladies, we must work hard. Too much time has been lost while your brothers were at home. I depend upon you to make up for lost time. Otherwise I shall not feel able to allow you to keep Horry."

The threat of losing their hearts' darling was a powerful goad.

"We will begin with your deportment," Belinda announced.

She sent them into the garden to pick sprigs of holly which she pinned to their dresses so the topmost leaves pricked their chins unless they held their heads high. She then balanced a book on each girl's head.

"Walk up and down, if you please, and do not allow the books to fall."

There was much groaning and muttering about the scratchy holly under their chins. The books tumbled off frequently.

"No wonder you are not successful," Belinda said
scornfully, "your steps are far too large. You are young ladies,
remember, not washerwomen."

She fetched tape from her workbox and tied Sarah's ankles
together, hobbling her, and then did the same for Kitty.

"'Miss Farrington, you cannot expect us to walk like this!"
Sarah cried. "I know I shall fall."

"Not if you take dainty steps as you are supposed to do.
Try a little harder." Belinda was merciless.

Kitty looked so mutinous that Belinda was obliged to
resort to bribery.

"Whoever allows her book to fall the least number of times
shall give Horry his supper."

Casting affectionate looks at their puppy asleep in his
basket they concentrated on achieving delicate steps. Once
they had acquired an elegant walk, Belinda said,

"You may untie the tapes now and practise going
downstairs."

"Not with the books and the holly!" Kitty wailed,
horrified.

"Indeed yes." Belinda was implacable.

"I shall fall and break my neck!" moaned Sarah.

"Flummery," said Belinda. "A lady has no need to look at
her feet. If you were coming downstairs in a beautiful ball
gown with a group of admiring gentlemen looking up at you,
I hope you would come down slowly looking at them, not
peering at your feet."

They grumbled, but they tried. There were many faulty
descents but when they had each come downstairs three times
without losing their books, Belinda said, "Excellent! That is
enough for now but I want you to walk for the rest of the day
as if the books and the holly were still there."

When they followed Belinda into the dining room at
dinner, they walked so sedately that Mrs. Sheldon was quite
startled and complimented them.

Next day they worked at stylish letter writing. Belinda

asked them to compose a letter of condolence to a friend whose mother had died, a letter of thanks for an unexpected gift and a graceful refusal of an unwanted invitation. She set a high standard and would not accept second best.

When the letters were at last finished and approved, Kitty threw down her pen with a sigh.

"That's that. What a horrid task, Miss Farrington. May we now take Horry for a run?"

"You may, but don't be too long, there is something else you must do before we are finished for the day."

When Horry had been taken out, the girls returned pink cheeked and bright eyed. They asked apprehensively what next they had to do.

"Now," she said, "you are to turn those charming letters into elegant French." She was deaf to their protests. "The sooner you write them, the sooner you will be free."

After much thought and pen chewing the task was complete and Belinda was pleased.

"There are one or two errors but you have done well. Now, remembering your deportment, go down and show them to your mamma. Straight backs when you curtsey, if you please and make sure you do not wobble."

Once again, Mrs. Sheldon was delighted. "What an improvement, Miss Farrington. Such lovely letters, so beautifully expressed and so neatly written. I should like to reward them with a treat. Mark shall take you and them for a picnic tomorrow, if you approve."

"That would be charming, ma'am, if Mr. Mark is not too busy."

"He shall make time to oblige me," said his mother majestically.

But when Belinda and her charges came down next day, ready for their outing, it was not Mark who was waiting to hand them into the barouche but Clive. Belinda had not done more than exchange cool courtesies with him since their angry exchange on the day of the bathtub incident and seeing him, her smile froze.

"Yes," he said in an undervoice, "I see you dislike this as much as I do but Mark was obliged to go to Woodbridge for Papa so Mamma insisted I should be your escort."

"It is a matter of indifference to me, sir, I shall not be discommoded by your presence." Belinda spoke coldly.

"Shall we call a truce, Miss Farrington, for the sake of the girls whose treat this is supposed to be?"

"By all means," she said stiffly as he handed her into the carriage.

Kitty and Sarah, looking happy, were already seated. Horry was clasped in Sarah's arms looking about him with interest.

Clive snorted. "You're not bringing a puppy on a picnic? He'll be a devilish nuisance."

"Don't forbid it, Clive," Kitty implored, "I'm sure he'll be good."

"He likes you, Clive," added Sarah, "he knows it is to you that he owes his good home."

Clive looked at Belinda who couldn't help smiling at this: his own expression was amused.

"Very well, but don't expect me to run after him."

Once more Horry healed a breach and the expedition got off to a better start than Belinda had anticipated. Clive talked affably about trivial matters that interested the girls and skilfully drew Belinda into the conversation. She began to thaw and before long, it was a cheerful party that bowled along the coast road. Then they met Frank Yardley.

He held up his hand and stopped the barouche. He came over, saluted and greeted each member of the party in turn.

"I wanted to enquire what happened about Master Will and the pressgang."

Belinda frowned. "He was released, no thanks to you, Mr. Yardley. Mr. Clive soon persuaded them of their error as you could easily have done had you been willing to help us."

Yardley looked disconcerted and there was an awkward pause until Clive said, "How is your campaign against the smugglers, Yardley? Any nearer to breaking up the ring?"

Yardley glared. "I know who is organising it: it is only a question of time before I get proof and can make arrests."

Belinda felt chilled. She felt as if the sun had gone in—but it still blazed above in a cloudless sky. She assumed Yardley was warning Clive. She darted a glance at him but he appeared in no way disturbed. Nonetheless, she shivered. Clive noticed.

"We must bid you good day, Yardley. We mustn't keep the horses standing and the ladies find this conversation little to their taste." He touched his hat and ordered the barouche forward.

When they were out of earshot he said, "Do I understand that Yardley refused to help you when Will was taken up by the pressgang?"

"Yes he did. He was odious!" Kitty said. "Miss Farrington asked him so nicely but Yardley was rude and crushingly unhelpful."

Clive gave Belinda a look of sympathy and, changing the subject, talked about Horry's training until they reached the spot he had chosen for their picnic.

The tide was out almost to the horizon exposing a vast expanse of yellow sand. At the distant water's edge they could see people and carts, tiny specks under the high, clear sky looking no bigger than children's toys. Belinda shaded her eyes to look at them.

"What are they doing, way out there?"

"Gathering seaweed to fertilise the fields, collecting cockles and clams or digging bait. Many people get their living working on the seashore," Clive told her.

"Including smugglers," Sarah added with relish. She never tired of talking about them. "Will says French boats sometimes drop weighted kegs at night for men to collect when the tide is out. They pick them up and hide them under the seaweed in their carts. Are they doing that today, Clive?"

"Will talks a deal too much," said her brother with a

frown. "Why don't you let Horry run? The wretched creature must be longing to stretch his legs after being clutched in your arms all the way here. Miss Farrington and I will stroll on the strand while you exercise your dog." Remembering her strictures on giving instructions to the girls, he consulted Belinda. "Is that agreeable?"

She smiled and nodded.

Kitty and Sarah needed no more encouragement, nor did Horry. As soon as he was set on the ground he began to run at high speed.

"Ventre à terre," said Sarah in delight, "his belly really is touching the ground."

The puppy ran in huge, wide circles away from the girls and back again, skidding and turning beside them and tearing off once more, describing great figures of eight, his ears streaming out in the breeze, his little pink tongue hanging out. His joy was catching and the girls jumped and clapped and laughed as they watched him. Then they began to run with him.

Belinda also found that joy was catching. Impulsively she turned to Clive and apologised.

"I'm afraid I behaved foolishly the other day, taking offence when, I am persuaded, none was intended. I shouldn't have taken umbrage at your laughter nor should I have spoken of you as I did to Mr. Mark. I didn't mean it—it was my temper speaking, I'm afraid. Will you forgive me, sir?"

Clive smiled at her making her insides flutter and her legs feel weak.

"That is as handsome an apology as any I ever received, Miss Farrington. But I should apologise to you. My laughter was unseemly, however tempting."

She looked at him sharply and saw his lips twitching and his eyes twinkling.

"Wretch!" she said and they smiled into each other's eyes, all constraint dissolved.

As they walked, to her great pleasure, Clive tucked her hand into the crook of his elbow. "I think I also owe you an apology for some hard things I said to you in the past. Being the eldest sometimes weighs heavily upon me. Much as I love my mother, I feel she is often more interested in social occasions and her flowers than in her children. I feel responsible for my brothers and sisters and have often been obliged to intervene when elderly governesses were ineffectual. "

"No wonder you spoke to me so severely when I first arrived."

"I did, didn't I?"

Belinda sighed. "I am afraid I am not an ideal governess: trying to tame your sisters has shown me what impertinence it was for me to have applied for the post."

"Nonsense, you are doing splendidly. Do you read Dr. Johnson? It was he who said, 'to strive with difficulties and to conquer them is the highest human felicity'."

"But I haven't yet conquered," Belinda said sadly.

Clive grinned. "The Doctor went on to say, 'The next highest is to strive and deserve to conquer.' You deserve success, dear Miss Farrington."

He stopped and turned to face her, standing close and looking down at her. It was at that moment when Belinda's heart was pounding and her feelings towards Clive were growing very warm indeed that Kitty and Sarah ran up and broke the spell.

"Horry is worn out and we are starving. May we eat our picnic now?" Kitty asked.

Clive grimaced at Belinda over his sisters' heads as he fetched the rugs and picnic basket. While they were eating chicken pasties followed by plum cake and washing it down with claret and lemonade, Sarah told Clive they had chased Horry to the water's edge.

"And do you know," she said, "the men were loading barrels onto their carts under the seaweed, just as Will said.

Isn't it exciting, I've never seen the Gentlemen at work
before."

Clive's eyebrows went up. "Were they indeed?" He
brushed crumbs from his breeches and rose to his feet. "I
think I'll just wander down and have a word: they may not
know Yardley is about."

Belinda said nothing as she watched Clive striding out
across the sands but her heart sank. Every time she decided
Clive was perfect and their relationship began to blossom, he
did something that made her sure he must be the Master-
smuggler. As he went to warn the men, her feelings towards
him cooled a little.

* * *

Later that afternoon when they had returned home,
Belinda was engrossed in a romantic novel when her peace
was shattered by Kitty and Sarah bursting into the
schoolroom in a distressingly unladylike way, agitated and
concerned.

"Miss Farrington," Kitty cried dramatically, "Horry has
been stolen!"

"We were taking him for a run before his supper and he
disappeared," said Sarah. "We whistled and called but he
didn't come even when we rattled his supper dish." This was
usually a powerful persuasion; for a little dog Horry had a
large appetite.

"He can't have gone far," Belinda said, "I'll fetch a shawl
and help you search."

They sought him in the formal gardens near the house, in
the shrubbery and by the lake, they looked in the
summerhouse and searched as far as the boundary wall.

"Have you tried the stables?" Belinda asked.

Sarah nodded. "We asked the grooms and the stable boys.
None of them has seen him. I'm sure he's been stolen and
will be held to ransom."

"I think that's a little dramatic," said Belinda. "Let's see if he has sneaked into the kitchens looking for tit-bits." They had had to retrieve him from cook's domain several times, but on this occasion he wasn't there. The girls were near to tears.

They met Clive in the hall. "What are these woe-begone faces for?" he asked in a teasing voice, "What terrible calamity has struck the schoolroom."

"Horry has been kidnapped," Sarah said, her voice doom-laden.

"Is this true, Miss Farrington?" Clive was grinning.

Belinda was reserved again having seen him warn the smugglers and was in no mood for Clive's teasing.

"We don't know that, only that Horry has disappeared."

"I suppose this notion of kidnapping comes from one of your lurid novels, Sarah," Clive said. "I imagine he has gone off on a private hunting expedition and will return in his own good time."

"But he's so little," wailed Kitty. "He may be lost and unable to find his way home. If only you had had that name plate made for him, Clive."

"You're making a Cheltenham tragedy out of a commonplace happening," said her brother loftily.

"Please go and look for him, Clive," said Sarah.

"What, and miss my dinner? He'll come home like Bo-Peep's sheep. Hadn't you better change? Mamma won't like it if you're late for dinner."

"Dinner!" shrieked Kitty, "how could we swallow a morsel while our darling Horry is missing? You're a monster, Clive."

He was close to laughter, his lips twitching. "Do you think so, Miss Farrington?"

Belinda was irritated. "No, but you are less than kind to your sisters."

"I am crushed," he said untruthfully with a wide grin, "but I'm dashed if I'll miss my dinner for a disobedient puppy."

The girls flounced off with Belinda behind them. On the stairs, they met Mark who waited politely on the half landing for them to pass. "Why the long, Friday faces?"

Belinda answered. "Their puppy is lost."

"We think he's being held for ransom," added Sarah.

"Good Lord! I thought that was a London crime. I had no idea there was a dastardly gang of dog thieves in the neighbourhood. May I see the ransom note."

"Now you're going to tease us like Clive did," said Kitty crossly. "He refuses to miss his dinner to search for him."

"How shockingly unfeeling." Mark shook his head sadly, but his eyes were brimming with laughter. "I shall have to save the family honour instead. But see they save me some dinner, I am starving."

"Darling Mark," Kitty threw her arms round him. "Best of brothers, will you really go?"

"If you find him, I'll embroider you some slippers," promised Sarah.

Mark's eyes glittered with mischief. "Tiny stitches or your usual huge ones?"

"Don't tease, sir." Belinda was struggling not to laugh. "How kind you are. We shall be thankful to think the search is in your capable hands."

"If I please you, Miss Farrington, that will be thanks enough." He gave Belinda a mocking bow and ran lightly downstairs and out of the front door.

"Now," said Belinda, "we must dress for dinner and do so quickly. Silver will ring the gong any minute now and we don't want to displease your mamma."

As she changed into a green gingham dress and threaded a green ribbon through her dark curls, Belinda compared Mark and Clive's treatment of their sisters: Mark's teasing had been good natured and he had gone to help while Clive's baiting had shown his arrogant streak and he had put his own comfort first. She was disappointed in Clive.

She went into the girls' room to assist with bows and sashes just as the gong sounded.

"Sarah! Why are you wearing that unsuitable black dress?"

"I'm in mourning for poor Horry."

Belinda wanted to laugh but she managed a frown. "Don't be so gothic, you look a perfect quiz. Change into your brown muslin with the blonde lace and hurry!"

She helped them with their fastenings and hair ribbons then led them downstairs.

"Heads up," she said bracingly. "Just because we are in the midst of a crisis, there is no reason to forget our deportment." Luckily she didn't see the hideous faces they made behind her back.

The family was waiting for them. Belinda apologised to Mrs. Sheldon for their delay and passed on Mark's message, explaining he was looking for Horry.

"More fool he!" said Clive, earning a haughty look from Belinda and glares from his sisters.

They were still on the first remove, the girls eating with their usual appetites in spite of Kitty's protestations, when the sky was rent by a flash of lightning followed by a deafening clap of thunder. All heads turned towards the windows upon which huge raindrops splashed.

"Poor Horry," Kitty cried, "he'll be so frightened all alone in a storm."

"Poor Mark." Mrs. Sheldon was more concerned for her son. "He'll be soaked."

Sarah burst into tears and ran to her mother, burying her head in Mrs. Sheldon's lap. Whether she was crying because the storm frightened her or because she was wrought up about Horry was not clear.

At that moment, Richard, the footman on duty in the hall, was heard to shout, "Hi!"

Through the doorway burst the bedraggled figure of Horry, his little black face and curly-haired body glistening with mud. Robert, the footman on duty in the dining room, made a dive for him and missed as Horry leaped onto Belinda's lap. He licked her face and generously shared his mud with her.

Another lightning flash and another thunder crash made the puppy flinch and he snuggled closer to Belinda. Her green and white gingham was now wet and stained.

"He's safe." Sarah ran to pet him, her tears drying up miraculously.

Clive laughed. "Graceless Scamp: it is just as I suspected, he's been rabbiting."

"Look at poor Miss Farrington's dress," Mrs. Sheldon said. "It's really too bad. You'll have to change, my dear. Give the dog to one of the servants to clean up."

As Belinda rose, Mark put his head round the door. "I admit defeat. Can't find the dratted dog anywhere and I'm soaked. I'm going to change."

"He's here, Mark," Kitty cried. "Wasn't he clever to find his way home?"

"He deserves the slipper." Mark's grin took the sting from his words.

"But you sir, deserve a medal," said Belinda lightly as she met him in the doorway. They smiled at each other.

Belinda handed Horry to Richard and as she and Mark walked companionably across the tiled hall towards the stairs, they exchanged grins again. Mark put his arm round Belinda's shoulders and said something in her ear that made her throw back her head and laugh.

From where he sat, Clive saw the exchange. His amusement died and he became very thoughtful. He stared at their departing backs, a frown on his face.

* * *

As Belinda washed her hands and face and changed into a fresh gown, she smiled, thinking of the trouble one little puppy could cause. She smiled again as she brushed her dark curls and changed the ribbon, remembering Mark's friendly arm round her as they mounted the stairs. She felt sisterly affection towards him: he was amusing as well as kind. He had not referred again to his offer which she was sure now had been nothing more than a tease.

Feeling light-hearted she began to descend the stairway from the schoolroom suite to the floor below. She was about to step out onto the landing when she heard Clive's voice and realised from the tone that he was scolding someone. She paused, not wishing to intrude on anyone's embarrassment.

"Don't think you can bamboozle me, Mark. You may fool everyone else but I know what you are up to."

"How clever and how pompous," Mark sneered. "But it's my life, brother dear, and I shall do with it whatever pleases me."

"You're shallow and irresponsible: your conduct is unworthy of a Sheldon."

Belinda stiffened, her eyes wide with shock. She knew what Clive was talking about: he was telling Mark to stop paying attention to a lowly governess! To cultivate her was irresponsible and unworthy conduct!

Utterly mortified, she picked up her skirts and ran back upstairs to the schoolroom where she pressed her burning cheeks against the cool window pane. Clive must have seen Mark's arm round her and disapproved.

How humiliating—yet she had nothing to be ashamed of: she had not encouraged Mark and in any case, although she was a governess, her papa was a younger son of Lord Farlow while the Sheldons had only money made in the east to give them consequence. Lady Anselm had told her to remember she was not inferior to them even though she was in their employ. Her chin went up, she would not allow Clive's odious words to upset her—nevertheless, she felt miserable.

After a while Clive put his head round the schoolroom door and when he saw her, he came in smiling. "Are you not coming down again? Mamma sent me to find you. Has horrible Horry quite spoiled your evening?" He sounded concerned and friendly.

"I have the headache, sir," she said coldly. "I shall sit here quietly for a while and then go early to bed. Please give my apologies to Mrs. Sheldon."

Clive looked concerned. "Poor Miss Farrington. Perhaps you had too much sun today at the picnic and the thunder can't have helped. I should like to sit with you but I'm persuaded idle talk will do you no good."

He smiled warmly and tiptoed away leaving Belinda more confused than ever. Clive had not sounded like a man trying to save his brother from her clutches. If she had not recognised his voice, Belinda would not have believed it was he who had uttered those scornful words. Now she really did have a headache.

Belinda slept badly that night. Her dreams were full of angry, ogre-like figures shouting at her that she was a silly, worthless chit.

Chapter Nine

The weather continued hot; the corn ripened to a burnished gold splashed with the brilliant scarlet of thousands of poppies. The harvesters descended on the fields, their sweeping scythes toppling the corn. The reapers' women gathered the fallen stalks and bound them into sheaves which were stacked in groups to await the carts that would take them to the barn. When this was done, the humble gleaners came into the fields, women and children who worked on hands and knees to gather up every last precious grain.

Harvest festival approached and Mrs. Sheldon again asked Belinda to decorate the church in her stead. Belinda readily agreed; she loved the smell of the church at harvest time when the scent of ripe apples mingled with the aroma of the newly baked bread that had been shaped into a loaf resembling a sheaf of corn, gilded yellow in its baking with beaten egg.

Belinda walked to the church, glad to be out of doors. As she passed the first house in the village, she saw that the white china cat in the window was facing the street so she was not surprised to meet Frank Yardley. She was too polite to ignore him although she would have liked to walk past with her nose in the air: she still had not forgiven him for his failure to help rescue Will.

When he saw her, he immediately dismounted to speak to her. He swept off his hat and bowed, his sallow face alight with pleasure.

"Miss Farrington, I am glad to find you on your own. Last time I saw you, you were with the Sheldons so I couldn't speak privately; I wanted to apologise for being unable to help you the other day."

"Unable, Mr. Yardley?" Belinda spoke scornfully.

"Unwilling more like. It was especially mean as I had helped you and kept the secret of your humiliation as I said I would. Why did you not help? Do you hate the Sheldons so much?"

He frowned. "You don't see that family as I do: I am convinced that one of them is the leader of the gang that it is my duty to catch. It's the devil's own job and I get no help from the local people. You who could be so useful to me, refused me your aid in that, remember. You wouldn't help me, so I didn't help you. But it was shabby and I apologise."

Belinda felt no sympathy for him but it would be undignified to quarrel. She inclined her head, accepting his apology.

Yardley brightened. "May I walk with you?"

She nodded reluctantly. "You may come as far as the church. I am going to help decorate it for the Harvest Festival."

Yardley walked beside her, leading his horse. He put his hand under her elbow which Belinda didn't like. "Have you thought any more about which of the Sheldons is the Master-smuggler?"

Belinda was exasperated. How tiresome he was, always harping on the same theme. "None of them," she said firmly, "you are quite out on that head, Mr. Yardley."

"So you say. Where were Mark and Clive last Thursday, the night of the thunder storm?"

"That is an impertinent question that you have no right to ask. But as it happens they were both at home. Why do you want to know?"

"It was pitch black after the storm and under cover of the darkness, four ships put in at Aldeburgh bringing contraband rum and tobacco. Later, the ships returned to Holland with a cargo of butter. Fishermen and farmworkers couldn't have arranged a run of that size: Clive or Mark must have set it up."

Yardley stared at her as if trying to see into her mind. Belinda's remembrance of that night was of Horry lost,

Mark's kindness in going after him and then Clive's harsh words to Mark about flirting with her. Neither of the brothers had gone out as far as she knew.

"I'm sure you are wrong, they are such an agreeable family."

They had reached the lych-gate that led to the churchyard. Yardley stood in front of Belinda barring her way and said, "Perhaps this is not the right moment but I must say something important." He cleared his throat nervously. "Will you do me the honour of becoming my wife, Miss Farrington? I have admired you from the first moment I saw you and I am tormented by the thought of you in the Sheldons' house.

"I am not rich, but I can afford to marry. I have a modest competence; fifty pounds a year from the Board of Customs and an annual allowance from my father of twenty-five pounds. We could be comfortable on that, couldn't we? If I break the Suffolk ring and catch the Master-smuggler I shall get promotion and my share of the goods seized. Please think it over Belinda, I love you and I want to get you away from Park Place before the day of reckoning."

Belinda was so stunned by this unexpected offer that she was momentarily bereft of words. Never had she thought of Frank Yardley as a possible suitor. She didn't like him at all. When she realised that he meant it, she drew herself up and said haughtily, "Marriage, Mr. Yardley what are you thinking of? We are no more than acquaintances. I find it hard to believe that you love me but if indeed you do, then I must tell you that I do not return your feelings."

"I do love you, Belinda, I do! You are beautiful and kind. Hardly a moment of the day passes that I do not think of you and wish you were by my side."

Belinda was not impressed. She had never been able to like Yardley, and his impertinence in approaching her in this way horrified her. For a moment she imagined what Lady Anselm would think of such a match and almost smiled. But her sense of outrage was stronger.

"You have a strange way of showing love," she said contemptuously. "You insulted me at our first meeting. Then you tried to make me spy for you. You were ungrateful when I rescued you and you refused to help me with Will. Friendship is out of the question let alone marriage and please don't think your offer gives you the right to use my Christian name."

"I'm sorry, Miss Farrington. Please don't be hasty; at least think it over. It would make me so happy if you could return my love." He was quite agitated now.

Belinda stared. How insensitive and uncouth he was to press her when she had already refused. To her dismay, he continued to plead, standing closer to her than ever.

"I am sure you will agree to my proposal when you have reflected. I may have spoken too soon—I should have liked to court you longer—but I am anxious to get you out of Park Place before the Master-smuggler is caught and you are compromised by living in the same house.

"We have caught one of the smugglers and in return for his freedom, he has given us information. He has told us that the next landing will be made tomorrow at Sizewell Gap. The Master-smuggler is sure to be there and this time I shall catch him. Please, Miss Farrington, leave Suffolk today or take tomorrow morning's stage; I don't want you involved."

"Thank you," she said distractedly. Her heart was hammering at this disquieting news. "I can't talk any more...I must think."

She turned away from the church and began to walk back to Park Place, decorating forgotten. The implication of what Yardley had told her was so devastating that she didn't give his proposal of marriage another thought.

That afternoon she sat in the schoolroom deep in thought, trying to devise a way to warn Clive without seeming to do so. Kitty and Sarah were working at their samplers and when they heard the distracted replies she gave to their questions, they giggled at her but she didn't even notice.

"Love," Kitty whispered to her sister, nodding sagely and they both giggled again.

Finally Belinda decided the best thing to do would be to mention it at dinner so it would be heard by the whole family and Clive would not know she had guessed his secret identity.

As she sat at table that evening, she toyed nervously with her food and then in a lull in the conversation she announced, "I met Lieutenant Yardley today in the village."

No-one was particularly interested except Kitty who was indignant. "Don't tell me he had the gall to speak to you?"

When Belinda nodded Kitty went on. "I'm surprised he dared do so after the shabby way he behaved over Will."

"He apologised for that," said Belinda hurriedly, trying to keep the conversation on the track she wished it to follow. "He told me he is now certain of success in breaking the ring. He plans to catch the smugglers tomorrow night."

Now she had the family's attention.

"Hmph," said Mr. Sheldon helping himself to green peas. "I've heard that tale before. Man's useless—not a good riding officer. Always arrives too late."

"How does he propose to catch them?" Mark asked.

"Apparently one of the smugglers has turned informer and has told him there's to be a landing at Sizewell Gap tomorrow night. He and his men will be waiting there with a squadron of dragoons."

"I hope he doesn't catch them," Sarah said.

"I own that I agree with you, Sarah," said Mrs. Sheldon. "Not because I approve of smuggling but because such a confrontation will lead to bloodshed and the imprisonment of poor men."

"Sentimental stuff! Just what I would expect from a female," said Mr. Sheldon. "Smuggling's unpatriotic—English gold helps Napoleon. French franc's worth nothing these days—debased. Boney is obliged to pay his troops in gold. Where does he get it? From English smugglers. Worse than that—spies use smugglers' boats to carry information."

"I'm sure our smugglers wouldn't have anything to do with spies," Mark said.

"What makes you think our smugglers are different from any others?" Clive asked his brother.

"Suffolk men are patriots."

"Rubbish. They're ruffians and cut-throats." Mr. Sheldon was in agreement with his eldest son.

"I wouldn't like to be in the informer's shoes," Clive said. "I'm afraid he'll suffer."

Mrs. Sheldon was distressed. "Please change the subject, I don't wish to hear about such things at my dinner table."

"Very well, m'dear, subject's closed," said her husband. "Pass the cherry tart."

Belinda had done her best: Clive was now warned but she was confused. Like his father, he had expressed disapproval of smuggling, but then, she supposed, if he were in deep, it was the line he would take. The more she knew about smuggling, the less she liked it. That spying might be involved had never occurred to her and she hadn't liked Clive's tone when he said the informer would suffer.

Next day, Belinda tried not to fret about what would happen at Sizewell Gap that night. She spent the morning teaching the girls the steps of a country dance.

"Your mamma will bring in a dancing master nearer the time of your come-out to teach you the latest steps, but if you know some already, it will save much time."

They pushed the furniture in the schoolroom back and she played the piano for them after she had shown them the steps. The Grand Chain made them giggle as they stepped round the room lightly, taking the hands of imaginary dancers

Horry found the dancing fascinating and climbed out of his basket to join in with joyful barking. He had to be banished to the stables where Tom, Will's erstwhile sparring partner, promised to keep an eye on him.

In the afternoon, Belinda, still anxious and restless, took the girls riding. They wanted to go along the coast road and see if anything was happening at Sizewell, but Belinda vetoed this and they rode inland. By dinner time, they were all pleasantly tired from the day's exertions and the girls ate with good appetites. Belinda didn't feel in the least hungry and had to be coaxed by Clive who sat next to her, to take a little chicken and some stewed plums.

After dinner, Belinda went up to the schoolroom to fetch some music for Kitty. She was going to play to show her mamma how much her technique was improving. Horry, who had scampered beside them on the ride, lay in his basket exhausted and slept peacefully. Belinda tiptoed out and closed the door quietly.

On the landing below she met Clive coming out of his room. He had changed from the blue coat, knee breeches and silk stockings in which he had dined and was wearing riding dress, his topcoat over his arm, his curly brimmed beaver in his hand. Belinda immediately felt alarmed, guessing he was going out to warn the smugglers.

He laughed at her shocked expression. "Yes, I'm creeping off, playing least in sight. Don't give me away, I beg. I'm going to a cock-fight at Saxmundham and Mamma would not approve."

"What you do, sir, is not my business," she said stiffly but she could have wept. Clive, of whom she was far too fond for her own good, was about to ride into danger.

In the drawing room she handed the music to Kitty and sat down, her thoughts in disarray. Mark came and sat beside her. Under cover of the music he whispered, "You're trembling, Miss Farrington, is anything wrong?"

She shook her head and tried to smile.

'"Did you see Clive upstairs? Is he to join us?"

"He was going out." Belinda tried to keep the despair she felt out of her voice.

"I hope he doesn't fall foul of Yardley and the excisemen."

Mark chuckled as if it were a good joke.

It was no joke to Belinda, she devoutly hoped so too. She had the gravest doubts about the cocking at Saxmundham.

* * *

By breakfast time next day, everyone knew that Yardley had failed again. Rumour said gloatingly that the excisemen had waited at Sizewell all night while the cargo was landed down the coast at Hollesley Bay, the Gentlemen having been warned. Belinda supposed sadly that Clive had done it when he went out last night. Yardley, gossip said, was in a terrible rage, vowing vengeance.

Belinda hoped Yardley would think the informer had played him false; she didn't want him to suspect that she had tipped off the Master-smuggler. Clive was safe this time but still she couldn't breathe freely, she would continue to worry until the moonlit nights returned: until then she knew the contraband would be hidden in all sorts of secret places until it could be distributed safely.

Kitty and Sarah wanted to ride again that morning, it was a beautiful sunny day so Belinda agreed. Kitty chose their route and elected to go through the village and out into the meadows beyond.

When Sarah saw the white cat in the window of the first cottage with its back to the street she grinned.

"We shan't meet Yardley today then."

"I wager he'll be too embarrassed to show his face," Kitty said.

"He will be searching for that cargo," Belinda said. "He might be anywhere."

Sarah said, "You understand smuggling now, don't you, Miss Farrington?"

Belinda smiled wanly, she wished she didn't. They rode along the narrow street that led to the church. They had to pass the cobbled square that was the heart of the village. It was the market place where farmers brought their fruit and vegetables, eggs and butter to sell and in the centre, it had a pump and horse trough, stocks and a pillory.

As Belinda and the girls approached, their horses' hooves sounded unnaturally loud. Although the square was crowded with people, they were silent, standing and staring at something. Their uneasiness was almost palpable.

"What is it?" Kitty asked.

Mounted as they were, they could see over the heads of the crowd to what held their attention. It was not a pretty sight, a man was in the pillory, his neck and wrists secured. His head lolled and his body sagged.

"I believe he's dead," Kitty whispered.

Belinda was about to say that was nonsense, but upon looking more carefully she saw that Kitty was right. The man's lifelessness showed not only in his slumped body and closed eyes; she saw to her horror that there was a notice pinned to his body by a dagger driven up to the hilt in his chest. Dark blood had trickled down over the placard.

"What does that notice say?" asked Sarah in a low voice.

"I can't see," said Belinda with a shudder she could not control. "Come away at once: this is no place for us."

A man standing on the edge of the crowd turned and answered Sarah's question.

"It says, TRAITOR TO THE BROTHERHOOD. That be the weasel that spilt on the Gentlemen. They never do forgive that. Do you goo home, young ladies. Miss is right—this ain't no place for you."

Belinda stared—the speaker was Jem the blacksmith. She needed no urging to go. She turned Warrior's head towards Park Place and made the girls follow her at a trot.

What she had seen shocked and frightened her. A man was dead because she had told Yardley's secret over the dinner table! The stark reality of smuggling struck her now as it never had before. This was like nothing in a novel, there was no romance in smuggling: it was cruel and ugly as well as being against the law.

If Clive was indeed the Master-smuggler, he was involved in this. She must not think of him with love as she had been doing. What would Papa have said? She had been too strictly brought up to be able to give love and respect to a man who broke the law and had blood on his hands. How could she love him?

Then her treacherous heart answered: how could she not love him? She could only pray she was wrong and that it was not Clive who controlled the smuggling.

* * *

Belinda was amazed at Kitty and Sarah's resilience. She still felt shaken and downcast. Although they had been quiet and pale on the way home, after nuncheon and their rest, they were quite restored. They had taken the violent death they had seen in their stride and were ready to continue life. For their sake, Belinda put her gloomy thoughts behind her.

She felt they needed a cheerful occupation so she chose dancing again. Attracted by the music, Mark drifted into the schoolroom and allowed his sisters to cajole him into partnering them. After a lively boulanger with Kitty he said, "Now, Kitty, you play a waltz and I'll dance with Miss Farrington."

Belinda frowned. "Certainly not, sir, we are not here to amuse ourselves but to learn. In any case I do not waltz."

"It's quite easy," said Mark, "Come, I'll teach you."

Belinda allowed herself to be persuaded. She knew the waltz was the rage in London although it had not reached the Assembly Rooms at Harrogate. She had never seen it danced and had heard it was rather shocking. As Mark took her hand and drew her close, smiling down into her eyes, she saw why. When he put his arm round her waist and pressed his hand into the small of her back, she felt it was unseemly to be so close to a man.

Muttering, "One, two, three—one, two, three..." Mark twirled her round the room. Belinda had a natural sense of rhythm and was a good dancer so she soon picked up the steps and followed his firm lead.

"That's enough," cried Belinda after a while, "I'm feeling quite giddy." Her cheeks were flushed and her eyes were bright. The girls were entranced at this glimpse of the wicked world outside the schoolroom.

At that moment Clive came in. "Oh-ho! So you waltz, do you, Miss Farrington?"

Belinda's heart sank. Was she about to suffer another of Clive's scalding set-downs? But that was not what he had in mind. "My dance, I think," he said, eyes twinkling. "Kitty, play that again."

He bowed to Belinda and put his arm round her as Mark had done but how different was Clive's touch as he drew her close and took her hand in his! The music began and Belinda moved, following Clive's lead. The extraordinary closeness and shared intimacy of the waltz, their bodies almost touching, was more disturbing than she had imagined possible. She concentrated on the behaviour of her feet so Clive would not notice the behaviour of her heart.

At the finish Clive bowed and Belinda dropped a deep curtsey.

"That was capital," he said.

"Am I not a good teacher? Better than a caper merchant." Mark grinned at his brother.

"Whatever is that?" asked Belinda laughing.

"I collect he means a dancing master. Had you not waltzed before today, Miss Farrington?" Clive was surprised.

She shook her head. "We were sadly behind the times in Harrogate."

Clive said, "The waltz is all very well in private houses, but not the thing for young unmarried ladies in public: remember that, Kitty and Sarah. You dance extremely well, Miss Farrington."

Belinda blushed at the compliment and to cover her confusion, sent the girls to the stables to fetch Horry, who had once again been banished. The brothers helped her put the furniture back in place and departed.

Belinda went to wash her face which was hot after her exertions and the astonishing feelings she had experienced in Clive's arms. It had been so heavenly that she almost forgot the ugly scene in the village that morning and her resolve to put Clive out of her mind.

When she returned to the schoolroom, Clive was there, leaning against a cupboard.

"That delightful dance made me forget that I came to thank you for not giving me away last night."

This brought Belinda down to earth; she spoke stiffly. "Did you enjoy the cock-fight, sir?"

"Not above half. I would rather have stayed and talked to you but I had promised to join friends and couldn't let them down."

Belinda concluded she knew what 'friends' he had joined.

Clive didn't seem to notice her coolness. "There was something else: I wanted to ask you if you are happy here? I was afraid you weren't when my sisters were behaving badly over the harum-scarum boys' departure."

Belinda could not stay aloof from Clive for long, especially when he showed such concern for her.

"That was a storm in a teacup, the kindness I have received from your family is more than I deserve, yet I am not persuaded I ought to stay here. I embarked on this career without giving it proper thought: having had a good education oneself does not necessarily mean one can impart one's knowledge to others."

"Very true, but no-one wants Kitty or Sarah to be a bluestocking—indeed it would be impossible. One cannot make silk purses from sows' ears."

Belinda smiled. "They are not that bad."

"I also wanted to congratulate you on the improvement

you have wrought in their manners and deportment. Their behaviour is now quite tolerable."

Belinda was pleased at this tribute but the girls gave it the lie by rushing wildly into the room chasing Horry.

"So much for that," Belinda said ruefully but Clive grinned.

"Would you look after Horry, Miss Farrington?" Sarah asked. "Mamma wants us in the conservatory and I dread to think what he'd do to her precious blooms."

"It doesn't bear thinking of," Belinda agreed. "Tidy your hair before you go, Sarah, you look like a gypsy."

"I must go too," said Clive. "I have to visit a family friend. I shall see you at dinner."

As Belinda tidied the schoolroom she was disarmed by Clive's charm and his concern for her welfare. If only she could rid herself of her conviction that he was the Master-smuggler she could be happy, but she could not give her heart to a criminal.

She opened the cupboard to put away the copybooks Kitty and Sarah had used earlier in the day. It was a deep cupboard, built into the wall, and ran from floor to ceiling with shelves at intervals all the way up. While the doors were open, Horry pushed his way forward and began to sniff the floorboards.

"Stop that." Belinda pushed the puppy back but he was on the scent of something. He evaded her hand and started to scratch at the boards.

"What can you smell? Not mice, I hope."

Horry began to dig.

"Silly dog, the floor's solid." Belinda knocked on the floor boards to show him. But it wasn't solid. The boards gave back a dull, hollow sound. "Horry, I do believe you've found something."

Belinda examined the boards. At the back there was a knot hole that looked natural but she found she could put her finger into it and lift the board like a trap door. There was a cavity below and in it were two parcels wrapped in tissue paper. Filled with curiosity she lifted them out and opened them.

The first was a bolt of lace, fine, white and cobwebby that must have come from Valenciennes. The second parcel contained heavy, ivory-coloured watered silk. As she stroked it, admiring the quality, she saw on the end of the board around which it was wrapped, the words Soie de Lyons.

Smuggled silk and lace!

She remembered who had been leaning on the cupboard when she came in earlier. The packages must have been put there by Clive who was indeed the Master-smuggler while she was out of the room washing.

With a heavy heart she returned the contraband to its hiding place and hugged Horry. She wished that neither she nor the dog had been so inquisitive. What should she do now? She decided there was only one person who could help her. She put Horry in his basket and went to find Mark—he would know what to do.

He was not in his room so she ran downstairs. The footman in the hall said Mr. Mark had gone into the garden not half an hour before, carrying fishing tackle. Belinda made her way towards the shrubbery, meaning to cut through it on her way to the lake.

As she approached the shrubbery, she heard somewhere within its depths, scuffling and a soft, feminine giggle. She paused and looked about her. Not far away, sitting in a grassy hollow, his back towards her, was Mark. She was about to call out to him when she realised he was not alone. Cuddled in the crook of his arm was Rosie, the upstairs maid. Mark was nuzzling her and kissing her. The giggling seemed to be because he had his hand up her skirt.

Belinda's cheeks flamed as if it were she who had been caught doing something indelicate. She stepped back quietly and fled hoping she had not been observed but Mark and Rosie were far too occupied to notice.

She could hardly believe it; Mark—seducing one of his

mother's maids! She had protested when Kitty referred to his lights o' love and when Simon talked of his flirts: was she the only person in the household who had not known what Mark was really like?

She began to see his attentions to her in a new light: she had believed he was fond of her and she had thought his warm looks denoted sincere admiration. How could she have been so naive—she had been no more than another female to flirt with. How galling to find herself on a par with a housemaid!

She ran through the garden as if trying to escape disillusion. Before long she came to the boundary wall where she stopped to catch her breath.

A figure stepped out from behind a tree, startling her.

"Miss Farrington!" a voice hissed. It was Yardley.

Furious at being surprised and by the riding officer of all people, Belinda spoke sharply. "What are you doing here?"

"Watching the house." He had a perspective glass in his hand.

"How dare you! Mr. Sheldon would be extremely angry if he knew. Go away, before anyone sees you."

Yardley snapped back at her. "Don't try to teach me my business. I suppose you heard that I missed the smugglers last night? The goods came into Hollesley Bay not Sizewell Gap. The wretch who informed was lying. Now I'm the laughing stock of the county."

Belinda felt no pity for him. "I suppose you know they killed the informer? I saw his body in the village this morning."

Yardley was angry and defiant. "It's not my fault—it served him right."

Belinda looked at him with distaste. "How can you say that when you forced him to inform. It was your fault."

Yardley glared at her. "It's of no consequence to me—one less ruffian to chase. I've got a warrant to search Park Place and, when it is dark and they are off guard, I shall do so. This time I'll find proof that the Sheldons are involved."

Belinda thought of the silk and lace in the schoolroom cupboard and wondered how many other hiding places in the house were crammed with contraband. She must warn Clive...

"Miss Farrington!" She jumped, aware Yardley was speaking. "Belinda—are you listening to me? Have you thought any more about my offer?"

How dare he! She couldn't believe he was so insensitive. She looked at him with loathing.

"I haven't changed my mind and I won't. Pray don't speak of it again, ever." She couldn't bear to be with him a moment longer, so repulsive did she find him. "I must go and change for dinner."

She hurried back to the house to warn Clive. She would have to come out into the open and speak of his secret; the very idea of doing so made her nervous.

She scratched on the door of his room but there was no reply. Greatly daring, her heart beating fast, she turned the handle and looked in. The room was empty.

She ran upstairs and changed quickly. In the schoolroom she sat down to write him a note. It wasn't easy to find the right words and she was dissatisfied with the result but time pressed and it would have to do. She twisted it into a billet and scribbled Clive's name on the outside and took it down to his room.

There was no reply to her knock. The room was still empty so she crept in and put the note near the mirror where he must see it when he changed. Evidence of Clive's occupation was everywhere: a row of gleaming boots on trees, a pile of freshly starched muslin neck cloths on his dresser ready for tying. The air was pervaded by the spicy smell of the Queen of Hungary's Water which he used on his hair. Belinda sighed and touched the shoulder of his blue coat lovingly.

As she came out, a voice behind her said, "So!"

She jumped like a startled foal. It was Mark.

"What were you up to in Clive's room?" he asked sternly.

The effrontery of this when she knew what he had been doing so recently almost took Belinda's breath away.

"How dare you question me, sir! I don't have to account to you for my actions."

He moved close and looked down at her and said in a low intimate voice, "Had I known you were flighty enough to visit men in their rooms, I'd have asked you to come to mine."

She felt her cheeks grow hot. "You, you..." Belinda couldn't think of a word bad enough to describe him.

Mark laughed and spoke in his usual voice. "Come now, Miss Farrington. I was only funning. You really must learn to take a joke."

"If that's your idea of a joke, sir, I cannot admire your taste." Belinda was still ruffled.

"In that case, I apologise. Why were you in Clive's room? I admit to being curious."

Libertine or no, she couldn't do without Mark's help.

"I can't tell you here. Come to the schoolroom. We shall not be disturbed, the girls are feeding Horry."

"I love secrets," Mark said gaily as he followed her upstairs, his light-hearted mood at variance with Belinda's fearful anxiety.

When they were seated she began. "I have for a long time suspected that Clive is the Master-smuggler." She told him her reasons—the barrel in the church, the fact that Clive was away from home every time there was a run and the contraband she had found in the cupboard.

Mark listened gravely but did not comment.

Belinda explained that she had revealed Yardley's plan at the dinner table in order to warn Clive and that when he had gone off, supposedly to the cockfight, she had surmised he was warning the smugglers.

"Now I have discovered that Yardley has obtained a warrant and is going to search Park Place tonight so I wrote a note to Clive to warn him," she finished. "That's why I was in his room.".

To her astonishment, Mark threw back his head and laughed.

"You silly little ninny," he said scornfully. "Your precious Clive is not the Master-smuggler—I am!"

Chapter Ten

Belinda's mouth opened in astonishment. Mark the Master-smuggler, not Clive? How could she have been so wrong? She shook her head.

"I don't believe you!"

Mark was in high good humour. "Well you may, for it's perfectly true! Clive has nothing to do with the Gentlemen at all. It is I who make all the arrangements. I sell the cargo and pay the men while Jem sees to the pack trains. He's the only one who knows that I'm involved."

Belinda still found it hard to believe. "But why, Mark, why are you involved in this ugly business?"

He shrugged. "I do it to fill my time and for devilment. It's not long since I was as harum-scarum as Will and Simon: I need excitement and I like the challenge.

"I didn't start it—don't think that: smuggling has been going on here for years. When I came down from Cambridge it was just small scale stuff run by Jem. I saw that it could be better organised and Jem was thankful to let me handle things. When I go to India, he will take over again and it'll go back to being a minor operation."

Belinda was stunned. It made her blush to remember the many times she had misjudged Mark and Clive. Papa had often said that her habit of jumping to conclusions would get her into trouble one day: it seemed that this was the day. What a wet-goose she had been. She was ashamed to think that she had been ready to condemn Clive because he had offended her sensibilities by upbraiding her when she first came to Park Place. It had been equally foolish to set Mark on a pedestal and to excuse him of possible involvement because of his easy manner and his apparent concern for her. She had not seen through the veneer to the shallow flirt the rest of the household knew him to be.

She still found Mark's revelations hard to believe and tried to justify the conclusions she had come to.

"But when Clive came into church that day when I was arranging flowers, and then Jevons moved the barrel, I was sure Clive was involved."

Mark was grinning. "Your mistake was to connect the two things. Clive was to read the lesson at the festival and went to check the passage. Jevons works for us occasionally, but Clive doesn't know. I kept telling you Clive had nothing to do with smuggling but you wouldn't believe me."

"But when we picnicked beside the beach, I saw him go to warn the seaweed gatherers that Yardley was about."

"That was pure kindness. He wouldn't want to see the villagers get into trouble."

"But it was Clive, not you who went out the night of the run to Hollesley Bay—I assumed he was warning the smugglers."

Mark shook his head, smiling at her naivety. "Clive went to a cockfight as he said. The trouble with you is that you make wrong deductions every time; I never knew such a girl for bad judgement. You thought I went to look for Horry on the night of the storm, didn't you? That's when I sent one of the stable boys with a message to Jem about the Aldeburgh run. You really are gullible."

Another of Belinda's illusions was shattered. "You didn't look for Horry?"

Mark was cheerfully unrepentant. "No, not at all. I'd never earn that medal you awarded me."

Belinda sighed. "You're wicked but you're clever: no-one in the house suspects you."

"Wrong again, Belinda! Clive is shrewder than you think. He knows. We had the deuce of a set-to the other evening. He gave me a fearsome trimming: said I'd have to give up—said it was conduct unworthy of a Sheldon."

Belinda's cheeks became hot as she recalled the interpretation she had put on the quarrel she had overheard.

"What about the informer—did you give orders for him to be killed?"

For the first time Mark stopped looking superior. He frowned. "No, nor would I. Jem arranged that, it's the code: all the men know that to betray the brotherhood means death. That's one of the reasons I'm going to give up being the Master-smuggler: that and what Papa said about spies using the Gentlemen. As far as I know, we've never carried information to the enemy, but I don't like the thought of it."

Although Belinda was hating herself for her stupid errors of judgement, she felt as if a great weight had been lifted from her: Clive was not the Master-smuggler; she no longer had to question his motives and could admire him freely.

"And it was you who put the silk and lace in the schoolroom cupboard?" she asked.

"Of course it was. And if Yardley's coming with a warrant I'll have to move them and several other packets hidden round the house. Drat the man. Why couldn't he take a bribe like the last riding officer?"

"You would offer him a bribe?" This was another shock for Belinda. She thought bribery was odious. She was beginning to see that being brought up by a clergyman was not the best preparation for living in the cynical, real world.

Mark said carelessly, "Yes it's done all the time. Most of them like to be greased in the fist. They're very badly paid, you know."

"Frank Yardley wouldn't take money from smugglers. He hates them because they harm his father's trade." Even though she didn't like the man, Belinda felt bound to defend his point of view.

Mark gave her a hard stare. "You seem to know a lot about him. You're not on his side are you?"

"How can you say that? Don't be nonsensical. Surely I demonstrated my loyalty when I told the family about his plan at the dinner table. I tried to warn the Master-smuggler, even if I was warning the wrong brother."

"That's true." Mark nodded. "Look, I must get this stuff away before Yardley comes with his wretched warrant. I've just thought of a famous plan, but it will only work with your assistance. Will you help me, Belinda?"

Belinda's first instinct was to refuse. She would have liked to go to her room to lie down with a damp cloth on her forehead and a vinaigrette in her hand while she tried to come to terms with these revelations. She was about to say no: then she thought what the disclosure of Mark's villainy would mean to the Sheldons. They would be disgraced and unable to hold their heads up in local society. All the family would be affected: Mrs. Sheldon who had been kind to her and Mr. Sheldon whose business might be ruined; it might have an effect upon the careers of the midshipmen; the girls might find it hard to make good matches if it were known they were sisters of a dastardly smuggler. Worst of all, her beloved Clive would be besmirched too. Perhaps by helping Mark she could repay the family's kindness and make amends for her stupid errors of judgement.

She said, "Do you really promise that you are giving up? That after this you will have no more to do with the Gentlemen?"

"Yes of course, but first I must get the goods away."

She sighed. "Very well then, I will help. Tell me what I must do."

"Good girl." Mark was in high spirits again. "Get out a paint box while I fetch some rice and order out the barouche. Have you got a bonnet with a veil?"

* * *

Clive had spent a boring afternoon visiting Sir Piers Elsdon, a family friend of long standing who was the local magistrate. The old buffer had prosed on about the political situation at home and the progress of the war abroad. He didn't like the news of Napoleon's march across Russia above half, he told Clive. He went on to fulminate about the high duties charged on imported goods, the inefficiency of Yardley, and then on to local affairs.

Clive had listened courteously, saying 'very true,' at frequent intervals even when he did not agree. Sir Piers was one of his father's oldest friends and Mark's godfather so Clive felt duty bound to be polite.

By the time Clive got back from Woodbridge, he had less time than he liked to dress for dinner but Jevons was an efficient valet and had everything ready for a quick change. It wasn't until he had finished tying his cravat in the tricky Trone d'amour that Clive noticed the note by the mirror.

"Where did this come from, Jevons?"

"I don't know, sir. It was here when I came up to prepare your clothes."

Clive opened it and read,

Sir,

It has come to my knowledge that Lieutenant Yardley has obtained a search warrant for this house and intends to execute it after dark today. I have discovered your secret and know that you are the Master-smuggler. I know that you have hidden silk and lace beneath the floor boards in the schoolroom cupboard. I beg you to dispose of it and other contraband before the search commences.

Please believe, dear sir, that I shall not refer to this matter again to you or any other person.

Your respectful friend,
Belinda Farrington.

* * *

Suddenly, many things became clear to Clive. He had been puzzled at Belinda's weather-cock behaviour towards him: one minute seeming set fair and next minute cold. If she had concluded he was the head of a gang of smugglers he could well understand her recoiling from him. He was a little miffed that she had been ready to believe such a thing of him but he hoped that once he had set the record straight, her warmer feelings would prevail.

He went off cheerfully to find her and on the way, he intended to drop a word of warning to his headstrong brother. He wanted but a few words with Belinda to set all to rights. He would scold her a little for her lack of faith and would reveal that Mark was the culprit. Once Belinda knew the truth, Clive decided he would tell her how he felt about her: it was high time she knew.

He knocked on Mark's door, opened it when he had no reply, saw that it was empty and went up to the schoolroom floor.

Clive was surprised not to find Belinda in her room dressing for dinner. He went next door and applied to his sisters. They were almost ready, helping each other with their sashes.

"I don't know where Miss Farrington is," Kitty said. "She may have gone down, but she usually waits for us."

Clive frowned. It was not like Belinda to neglect her charges. He went downstairs deep in thought. In the hall Clive met the butler.

"Silver, have you seen Miss Farrington or Mr. Mark?"

"They've gone out together, sir. Mr. Mark ordered the barouche an hour ago. I understand they are not dining at home."

Clive's frown deepened. In the drawing room, his mother, serene in a gown of coffee-coloured lace, was glancing through the latest edition of La Belle Assemblée waiting for the family.

Clive made a lightning decision.

"My apologies ma'am. I shan't be joining you for dinner—old Sir Piers insists I eat my mutton with him. I only came home to change."

Mrs. Sheldon smiled tranquilly. "How tiresome for you dear, but you are right not to offend such an old friend. My table will be very thin of company this evening: Mark has escorted Miss Farrington over to visit Lady Barton, Lady Anselm's friend—another arrangement made at short notice. Papa and I will have to make do with Kitty and Sarah's company."

Clive did not for a moment believe Belinda and Mark's invitation and wondered what prank Mark had embroiled Belinda in. He sent Richard, the footman, to tell Jevons he wanted his driving coat and hat and made for the stables where he called for his curricle. Ben, the undergroom, set about harnessing Clive's matched greys quickly and efficiently.

"I understand Mr. Mark has taken the barouche?"

"Yessir," Ben said.

"Is Foster driving him?"

"No sir. He's drivin' hisself."

"And Miss Farrington's with him?"

"Yessir, leastways, I think 'twas her, sir. Couldn't be sure. The veil she was wearing was that thick."

Clive's eyebrows rose. He deplored gossiping with servants but for once, it was necessary.

"Wearing a thick veil, was she? Odd on such a warm evening."

Ben grinned. "Yessir and what's even odder, Mr. Mark, he borrowed Foster's driving coat and hat. A rare old coachman he made. We all had a good laugh."

Clive smiled thinly. "A practical joke, I collect. Both in disguise to surprise someone."

"Yessir."

"Which road did they take? I've a mind to catch them up and join in the prank."

"Miss mentioned Ipswich, sir."

Clive took his coat and hat from Jevons who had come running out into the yard with them. He climbed into the curricle and signalled to Ben to spring the horses and swept out of the yard.

He had checked the false bottom of the schoolroom cupboard, the existence of which he had not hitherto known. It was empty and he guessed that Mark had put the goods in the hiding place under the seat of the barouche originally designed to foil highwaymen.

Why had Mark taken Belinda as his passenger? Why was she heavily veiled? He was angry with Mark for involving her and intended to have a sharp word with his brother when he caught up with them.

When he got to the post road, Clive could not decide which way to go: Ben said Belinda had mentioned Ipswich but that was not a certain indicator. Probably Mark intended to hide the contraband at a safe house. Unfortunately he had no idea where Mark's acquaintances lived.

The roads were dry and dusty so he saw no hoof prints or wheel marks to give him a clue. He sighed and set off towards Ipswich.

* * *

Belinda was surprised by Mark's plan but his enthusiasm overcame her doubts: it was a mad scheme but it might just work and the danger would be worth it if she could save the Sheldons from disgrace.

She looked in her wardrobe for a suitable costume for the escapade and decided on the dress she had worn for Isabella's picnic. It was no longer smart; the removal of the dog's bloodstains had left marks on the buff silk. Miss Lally, Mrs. Sheldon's dresser, when consulted, had sniffed and said it was ruined and should be thrown away but Belinda had put it in the back of her cupboard and was glad now that she had kept it. She carried the rose coloured pelisse over her arm in case it was cold later and added a heavy veil to the matching bonnet, as Mark had requested.

After looking in her mirror, she went into the schoolroom where Mark was making his preparations.

"Look at me," she cried, "I look a quiz and an antidote in this veil."

Mark tried not to laugh. "Don't be vain, Belinda. What does it matter how you look?"

She glared at him. "Do not use my Christian name like that, it is over-familiar."

Mark shrugged. He was equally unhelpful in the stables. After he rigged himself out as coachman and joked about it with Foster and Ben, she begged him to put the hood of the barouche down as the evening was sultry.

"What a wet-goose, you are, Belinda! We want concealment, not display."

"It's all very well for you," she retorted in an undervoice so that Ben could not hear, "you chose this wretched adventure, I did not! I have to sit above a cavity crammed with run goods. If we're caught, I'm as vulnerable as you to the penalties of the law. What they do with female smugglers, I don't like to imagine."

Mark laughed unsympathetically and drove off. He was in high spirits but Belinda was not: she was uncomfortable lurching and swaying over the rutted side road Mark had chosen, and she was stifled by the veil and the closed carriage.

After they had driven some way, the jostling and jolting suddenly stopped abruptly. She peered through the window and saw a rustic in a smock talking earnestly to Mark, but to her annoyance, she couldn't hear what was said. It seemed urgent and important from the way the man waved his arms and as soon as he had finished speaking, he scuttled away.

As the coach began to turn laboriously she put her head out of the window. "What's happening?"

Mark leaned down from the box. "We've got to go elsewhere. Fred says Drover's Farm is surrounded by excisemen: they must have learned that it was one of my safe houses from that dratted informer."

"Where will you go now?"

Mark did not reply. He was fully occupied turning the barouche in the narrow roadway. When he had finished he spoke testily. "Let me worry about that. My part is to do the driving and yours is to sit still. Don't forget what you have to do if we're stopped."

Before Belinda could protest, they were under way again and after a while, she realised from the smoother ride that they were on the post road. This agitated her. She didn't like being entirely in Mark's hands for she was not convinced of his competence. After a while, she rapped on the roof and when Mark slowed down she put out her head again.

"This is madness, Mr. Mark. This is the main post road from Ipswich. You said we would only make a short journey along back roads. This is far too public, we shall be recognised."

"What a nag you are, Belinda! I know what I'm doing, thank you. I've run the smuggling operation for more than half a year without your advice and I don't need it now. The post road is so busy we'll be lost in the crowd; that thick veil disguises you and no-one looks at a coachman."

"Could you not throw the contraband over a hedge and go home? Yardley will have finished searching by now."

Mark was indignant. "Throw it away? I should just think not! We're going to Beccles to a safe house."

"But that's miles!" Belinda was appalled. "It'll be dark by the time we get there."

"'So it will if you don't stop talking—you're a regular jaw-me-dead! Be quiet and let me drive!"

The barouche lurched forward and Belinda toppled back in her seat feeling thoroughly hard done by and not at all reassured.

Mark's airy notion of the post road being so busy that they would escape notice was wrong. Just as Belinda had feared, after a few miles, a couple of excisemen stepped into the road and halted the coach. Luckily they were not local men who would have recognised the Sheldon turn-out.

"Sorry matey," a little cockney said to Mark, taking him for the coachman he was pretending to be. "We've orders to stop all coaches and search them. There's a big operation on tonight to catch some smugglers."

Belinda's heart was beating fast. She heard Mark say calmly in a thick Suffolk accent, "You'm welcome to search if you hev a mind to, but mind you don't catch something worse than smugglers! I'm a'takin' the young lady in there to the fever 'orspital. She's got smallpox."

The first exciseman was taken aback but the second one said, "Garn, that's a likely tale! Ain't you afeard o' catching it?"

"Not me," said Mark, "I've had that but do you tek a look at her."

The door of the barouche opened but the excisemen showed no inclination to step in nor to ask Belinda to step out. Through her thick veil, Belinda saw worry on their faces.

"Oh sirs," she said in a feeble voice, "pray don't stop us. I am exceedingly poorly and must get to the hospital quickly." She lifted her veil to show her face which was covered with scarlet blotches and pimple-like excrescences.

There was a sharp intake of breath and the excisemen stepped back and quickly closed the door.

"That's smallpox all right," said the little cockney. "I seen it afore. I ain't going to search. Drive on, coachman."

The barouche moved again and Belinda sighed with relief. She hadn't believed that sticking grains of rice to her skin and painting them to simulate smallpox pustules would work, but Mark was right. Most people were so terrified of the disease that they would not want to look closely.

They had been making good speed and eating up the miles as they bowled along smoothly and Belinda began to think all would be well, but then she noticed their pace was slowing and she could hear the horses' gait was ragged. She put her head out.

"Is something wrong?"

"Confound it, yes. One of the horses has gone lame. We'll have to go to a post house for another horse."

"If we must go to an inn, do let's get something to eat. It's long past dinner time and I'm hungry."

"Don't be such a gudgeon. You can't go into a posting house. You're supposed to have smallpox. Besides, I need you to stay in the coach and sit tight on that stuff. We don't want nosy grooms and postboys looking in."

Belinda had no intention of doing any such thing: she was sick of the whole enterprise. "Let's have an end to this hare-brained scheme, Mr. Mark. I don't want to go to Beccles—after we've got the fresh horse, let's go back to Park Place."

"We dare not. Even if the search is over, I'll lay a monkey there'll be excisemen and dragoons all round the house lying in wait. We can't go back until tomorrow."

Belinda was furious. "You don't mean to keep me out all night? What of my reputation?"

"We'll say Lady Barton asked us to stay. I'm not going home until this cargo is safe. It represents my spending money for India. There's a post house about a mile ahead, I'll lead the horses. Sit there and don't complain."

* * *

The evening was warm and although it was eight o'clock, it was still light and many travellers were yet on the road. The yard at The Black Bull was seething with coaches, chaises, ostlers and postboys when Mark led the barouche in. After a consultation, he came and spoke gloomily to Belinda.

"We'll have to wait for a change of horses."

"In that case, I'm going in to wash this paint and rice off my face."

"You can't, we might be stopped again."

"I'm going to," Belinda said firmly. "I'm hot and the paint

is running. I'm going in and what's more, I'm going to have some supper."

Mark was annoyed at Belinda's show of independence. "Tiresome girl! But now, you remind me, I'm famished. I'll come too: we'll take a private parlour."

Belinda went in and spoke to the landlord. A maid took her up to a chamber where she could wash and tidy herself. She had just gone upstairs when Mark came in and addressed the innkeeper in lordly fashion. He had quite forgotten he was dressed as a coachman.

"Supper for two in a private parlour and look sharp about it."

The host bristled. "Round the back!" he shouted. "What are you about, ordering private parlours and suppers as if you was an Earl? The taproom's the place for coachmen!"

A young man who was paying his shot observed this exchange with interest. His languid air, his startling waistcoat, his beautifully tailored coat, his high collar points and his quizzing glass with a jewelled handle proclaimed him a rich man and a dandy. He put up the glass and studied Mark whose face was reddening with indignation.

"Good God—it's Sheldon!"

Mark jumped and pulled Foster's tricorne down over his eyes. "No it's not," he said gruffly.

"Can't fool me," said the dandy smugly. "Know you anywhere. What are you doing here, Sheldon, and why are you dressed as a coachman?"

"Because he is one, sir," said the landlord who had taken Mark in strong dislike, "and a damned impertinent one too, begging your honour's pardon."

"That he is not! Think I can't recognise a fellow who had rooms next to mine—coachmen don't go to Cambridge. As sure as I'm the Honourable Damian Horsford, that's Mark Sheldon."

The landlord looked disbelieving. "Ho, Cambridge is it? Then why is he dressed like a coachman?"

Damian Horsford put up his quizzing glass and inspected Mark again. "Yes, why are you, Sheldon? Dashed bad ton going round dressed as a coachman."

Mark realised he was in trouble. What bad luck that he should meet Horsford who was as inquisitive as a truffle pig and a gazetted gossip-monger. He spoke in a low voice. "Look here, Horsford, can't tell you in public—it involves a lady's honour. Make the landlord give me a private parlour and I'll spill the beans."

The Hon. Damian's free-spending ways had endeared him to the landlord so it needed no more than a nod to get them installed in a snug little parlour where Mark thankfully threw off Foster's coat and hat revealing his own neat clothes.

"That's better, dear boy. Now you look more like yourself. Now tell me your deadly secret—I won't blab."

But Mark knew he would, so he spun Damian a yarn. "Fact is, I'm eloping with an heiress. Did you see a young woman in a heavy veil come in? That's the heiress. When she joins us, I beg you won't mention the elopement, she's shy about it."

"Well, if that don't beat the Dutch!" Damian's eyes sparkled. This unexpected piece of information made the dull week he had spent visiting a tiresome uncle worth while. "Of course not, dear boy. Rely on me. Got a special license? Have to have one, you know."

"Er, no. In fact, that's where we're going—to Norwich to get one from the Bishop." Mark was pleased with this improvisation.

"That's all right and tight then. Rich, is she?"

"Fantastically." Mark rolled his eyes. He was spared further details as at that moment a maid came in with a steaming pot of coffee, a large ham and a plate of thin bread and butter. Mark fell upon the food as if he hadn't eaten for a week.

Belinda, much refreshed after removing the paint, the rice and the veil, came into the parlour. He stopped, surprised to see a stranger.

Both men stood up. Mark introduced them.

"Ma'am, this is the Honourable Damian Horsford with whom I was at college. Damian, this is the lady I mentioned."

Damian bowed over Belinda's hand. "Your servant, ma'am. Be assured I'll do anything in my power to help the enterprise."

Belinda was startled by Damian's effusiveness. She assumed from his words that he was something to do with the smuggling ring.

"How do you do, sir," she said politely and sat down. She helped herself to coffee and tucked into the bread and butter while Mark demolished a huge plate of ham. Damian prattled to Mark about mutual acquaintances while they ate.

After a bit, Mark sprang to his feet. "Can't sit here jawing all night, Horsford. We must be on our way. I'll settle the bill and meet you in the yard, Belinda."

Serenely unaware of the shocking lies Mark had told Horsford, Belinda shook hands with him and said farewell. When she had gone, Mark said, "I need hardly ask for your silence."

Damian smirked. "Secret as the grave, old lad. What a beauty your heiress is—I wish you happy."

As Mark walked out to the yard he guessed Damian would spread the tale of his elopement as soon as he could, but reflected that as there was no truth in it, it would do little harm.

But Mark was quite wrong.

Damian decided it was too late to go on that night and went into the taproom for a glass of claret. He was wondering how he could use the scandal he had garnered when Clive walked into The Black Bull.

Such was the elegance of Clive's appearance and so commanding was his manner that the landlord elbowed the tapster out of the way so he could serve the newcomer himself.

Clive had had a trying evening. He ordered a pint of

home-brew to clear the dust from his throat and drank it down before questioning the landlord.

"I'm looking for a young relative of mine, a very shy person wearing a heavy veil. Has she been here this evening?"

The landlord was immediately on the defensive. "What if she has? Nothing wrong, I hope."

Clive was reassuring. "No indeed. I had planned to meet her further south but was held up. I thought she might call here for refreshment."

"Well she did. The lady was all right but there was something havey-cavey about her coachman. He was dressed like one but said he wasn't. I'd have thrown him out but this gentleman here vouched for him, said he was at Cambridge with him. I ask you sir, I didn't cut my eye teeth yesterday. Whoever heard of a coachman getting an eddication?" He sniffed his disbelief.

Damian was deeply interested. Was this a jilted lover or an irate brother? The incident got more intriguing by the minute. He stepped forward.

"The Honourable Damian Horsford at your service, sir."

Clive smiled and held out his hand. "Clive Sheldon. I collect you were up at Peterhouse with my brother Mark?"

Not the lady's kinsman but Sheldon's brother! This flustered Damian and he began to babble.

"Yes—I mean, no. It wasn't Sheldon... Yes it was. Saw him but he wasn't with a lady."

Clive stared. "Mark was here, dressed as a coachman but not with a lady? Did you see the veiled woman the landlord mentioned?"

"Yes—I mean, no!" Damian hopped from foot to foot like a fly in a tar box. "Not the heiress—lady was on her own. Someone else."

"The heiress?" It was Clive's turn to be floored. "Don't you mean governess?"

"Haw haw, governess!" Damian laughed heartily. "Now you're bamming, trying to pull the wool over my eyes. But I know! Your brother confided in me. If he wants to marry the lady and she's rich, why try to throw a rub in his way?"

"Rich?" Clive was astounded. "Poor as a church mouse, more like. Marry? No such thing! Mark was having you on, he's a dab hand at pitching the gammon." Clive shook his head.

Damian was nettled. "Think I can't tell a smoky tale from a true bill? They're off to Norwich to see the Bishop—special license. He called the lady Belinda, if you want to know."

Clive glared at Damian as if he would like to throttle him. It was at this moment when he was scowling murderously that he was astonished to see a familiar figure sail down the stairs. It was Miss Isabella Hallingbury.

"Clive," she gushed, "how perfectly delightful to meet you here and how unexpected. Yet, I don't know. When I saw your sisters' little dab of a governess upstairs, I wondered what she was up to. Now don't tell me, let me guess," she simpered. "I know. She's run off with the family silver and you are in pursuit. How shocking! I never did trust her."

Clive's face was like a thundercloud. "Nothing of the sort, Isabella, she is with Mark and we had all arranged to meet. I learn I have just missed them. But how do you come to be here?"

"It is the most tiresome thing. I've been visiting an aunt in Norwich and on the way home we broke a trace and had to stop here. Aggravating—this is not one of the best post houses."

Clive murmured something sympathetic but he was more interested in Belinda. "Did you indeed see Miss Farrington here?"

"It was certainly her, she was wearing the dress she wore at my picnic, the expedition that was spoiled by her shocking behaviour. I couldn't think why she was here."

Damian had enjoyed the exchange. He could contain himself no longer and said with a grin, "She's making a runaway match with Mark Sheldon. Allow me to introduce myself, the Honourable Damian Horsford at your service, ma'am."

Isabella looked him over approvingly and gave him her best smile. "Isabella Hallingbury," she simpered holding out her hand. "Do tell me more. The governess running away with Mark—how outrageous." Her expression belied her words showing deep enjoyment.

"Did you say governess, ma'am, not heiress?"

"That chit an heiress? What a suggestion. No indeed, she is a governess. Now, I am an heiress."

Damian and Isabella looked so pleased with themselves that Clive, who they ignored completely, snorted in disgust. "I assure you both that you have the wrong end of the stick. This incident has nothing to do with marriage, runaway or otherwise. And now if you'll excuse me, I must be off."

His remark fell on deaf ears. Isabella and Damian hardly noticed his departure, so deep were they in conversation and absorbed in each other.

Clive walked out fuming. Horsford and Isabella were both vulgar gabsters: now irresponsible gossip would spread all over the county and further, he guessed, if Damian had his way. Justice would be served, he thought, if those two made a match of it—they were equally odious.

What nonsense to suggest Mark and Belinda were to be married. He knew very well that Mark had thought up some mad scheme to get the contraband away from Park Place; Belinda's note proved it.

But as he climbed up into his curricle, doubt began to creep in. Silver had told him Mark had sent for rice. Ben said Belinda was wearing a veil. Veils and rice spelled weddings.

Clive felt a sudden chill.

Chapter Eleven

In high summer, the evenings are light until quite late but by the time Mark and Belinda took the road again, daylight was finally fading. Stars were already spangling the sky and the moon was like a silver nail paring. Mark was driving at a good pace through the dusk. Belinda, carried along against her will in the swaying barouche began to feel sleepy and long for journey's end.

In the yard of the posting house Mark had told her they had not much further to go.

"But what are we going to do when we have delivered the goods?" she had asked. "We shan't be able to turn round and come straight back, I suppose."

"No, of course not. Don't be such a goose. We'll wait until morning."

She protested again about the impropriety of staying out all night.

"Don't get in such a pucker. It's a perfectly respectable farmhouse. The farmer's wife will look after you."

"How can it be respectable when it's a receiving house for stolen goods?" Belinda said indignantly.

"Don't be missish, Belinda. I thought you had more spark and spunk."

Belinda had given up arguing and got into the barouche. As it bowled along the post road in the twilight, she fell into a light doze, exhausted by her long day. The next thing she knew, she was awakened by a loud shout and the barouche stopped.

She peeped out of the window and was aghast at what she saw. This time there was little chance of talking their way out of trouble for standing at the head of a little knot of uniformed excisemen was Frank Yardley holding a lantern high and peering up at Mark who he did not seem to recognise.

"Come down, coachman, while my men make a thorough search of your vehicle. Are you carrying passengers?"

Although Belinda knew that it would not be long before all was discovered, she felt strangely calm. She pulled her veil down and waited.

Mark was still trying to make the best of the situation. "There be a sick young lady in there, sir," he said in his Suffolk accent. "She hev the smallpox, I'm a'takin' her to the fever 'orspital—you leave her be."

"That won't worry me, I had it as a child," said the riding officer crisply, "no-one gets it twice."

He opened the door and leaned in. "This won't take a moment, ma'am." He spoke politely, still not realising who he had stopped. "I am afraid I must search the coach. Are you well enough to stand?"

Belinda had a curious sense of déja vu: it was exactly like her first day in Suffolk, Yardley had asked her to stand up then.

It was when she stood up that something about her must have alerted Yardley in spite of the heavy veil. He thrust the lantern close to her face, tugged at her veil pulling her bonnet awry.

"Miss Farrington!" he gasped, visibly shocked. He whirled round and knocked Mark's hat off. "Mark Sheldon! I might have known. Hold him!" he snapped.

As two of his men took Mark by the arms, Yardley dragged Belinda out and jumped into the barouche. He lifted the seat cushions and found what he was looking for in the cavity below them.

"At last, I've caught you red-handed!" he crowed. "Didn't I always say I would, Sheldon? You're both under arrest."

"Don't be a fool, Yardley." Mark resumed his own personality and spoke contemptuously. "You can't arrest Miss

Farrington—she is innocent. She didn't know the goods were there, she just came with me for company."

Belinda opened her mouth to protest but was quelled by a look from Mark.

"If that's true, it will all come out when you are examined by the magistrate. But for the time being, you are both under arrest. You'll both be taken to the nearest lock-up."

This made Mark furious. "My God, Yardley, even you with your crass lack of manners wouldn't put a gently-bred girl in a common lock-up."

Yardley's face was pale in the flickering lantern light. "I can and I will!" he said grimly.

* * *

Clive drove as fast as he could safely go in the diminishing light. By parting with a guinea, he had discovered from the grooms at The Black Bull that the barouche was less than an hour ahead of him and was heading for Beccles. His generous tip had produced him the best pair of horses available. He was determined to overtake Mark and Belinda before they stopped for the night.

His face was grim: he had expected to find the feckless pair he sought disposing of contraband which was bad enough, but his conversation with Damian Horsford had made him furiously angry. He couldn't bear the thought of Mark and Belinda marrying; it would be a most unsuitable connection.

This turn of events had shaken him. He had thought Belinda cared for him and was chagrined that she should have succumbed to Mark's flashier charms. He had seen there was affection between his brother and Belinda on the night of the storm when Horry was lost but he had thought it was another case of Mark not being able to resist a pretty face. He had thought Belinda would see through Mark and reject him but she was trusting and, he discovered, very dear to him. Mark was a flirt, something he might grow out of, but Belinda needed someone to care for her and protect her, something he was willing and able to do. He cursed himself for the times he had used angry words to her and perhaps alienated her.

Even if he couldn't have her himself, he was determined to save her from an unhappy marriage with his brother. He tried to tell himself his motive was altruistic but he was devilishly jealous of Mark.

It was as these thoughts were occupying his mind that he came upon the extraordinary tableau of the excisemen and their prisoners in a pool of lantern light. Cursing under his breath he pulled up his horses and jumped down from the curricle.

What was Clive doing here, Belinda wondered as she saw his tall figure striding up: then she remembered with a start the note she had left him. In her surprise at Mark's revelation and the bustle of their departure, she had forgotten to remove it from his room. She blushed thinking of her idiocy but no-one noticed her scarlet cheeks in the flickering lantern light: all eyes were on Clive.

He strode up to Yardley. "What's going on here, Yardley? Why are your men holding Miss Farrington and my brother?" His voice was tight with anger.

A crooked smile appeared on Yardley's face and he almost purred. "Another Sheldon! How interesting! You are both involved, I assume. Search the curricle," he ordered sharply.

Clive shrugged. "Do by all means, I've nothing to hide."

The excisemen searched but found nothing. Yardley was disappointed.

"Unfortunately, the law doesn't allow me to arrest you on suspicion, so you can go this time. But your brother and Miss Farrington were caught in possession of run goods, so they will be taken to the lock-up."

Clive stared. "You intend to take Miss Farrington in charge? By God, you shall not."

"That's what I said, Clive," said Mark. "Look here, Yardley, if I confess to running the smuggling ring, will you let Belinda go?

"No." Yardley was calm and defiant. "Even if she's innocent, she is a material witness. I cannot free her in case she absconds."

Belinda had kept quiet until now, but this was too much for her. She was irritated that the three men should stand there discussing her fate as if she were a parcel to be disposed of.

"Frank Yardley, you are despicable! You have no idea how to treat a lady. This is the second time you have refused to help me although when you were in need, I gave you my help freely and without conditions. You profess you love me but you refuse to trust me. How dared you speak of love: it's obvious that you never loved me, for love and trust go hand in hand. Thank goodness I didn't entertain your offer of marriage for a moment."

Clive and Mark swung round and stared at her. "Marriage?" Mark was incredulous. "He had the effrontery to make you an offer?"

"What?" said Clive who was equally outraged, "you never mentioned it."

Belinda's temper was rising. "Why should I, it was no-one's business but my own. He only asked me to get me to spy on you and Mark."

"You know that's not true," Yardley cried, his face contorted with emotion.

One of the excisemen nudged the man next to him and muttered, "This here's as good as a play."

"Did he really ask you to spy on us?" Clive asked.

Belinda nodded. "I refused, of course."

"You're even more of a blackguard than I thought!" Clive said contemptuously.

"It'll be no good questioning Miss Farrington," Mark said to Yardley, "She's going to marry me, and wives can't give evidence against their husbands."

"Marry you?" Yardley was taken aback.

"Yes, I offered for her ages ago."

Belinda spun round. "No I am not! What makes you think I'd marry you, Mark Sheldon?" she said angrily.

"Of course you will," said Mark complacently, using the smile that had melted hearts and opened doors for him all his life. "You've been throwing out lures to me for ages. I could see you liked the idea when I asked you down by the lake and you have been telling me all evening that I have compromised you, so you'll have to marry me. Anyway it'll be a sight better than being a governess and you'll like India."

Belinda stamped her foot. "I won't marry you, no matter what you say and I've never cast lures in my life. You need not fear I shall bear witness against you, but for your family's sake, not yours."

"Belinda." Clive, ignoring the interested spectators, took her hand and said gently, "were you not running away to marry Mark?"

Belinda looked up at him and her voice softened. "Of course not. How could you think so?"

Mark began to laugh. "Don't tell me you fell in with that incurable gossip Damian Horsford?"

Clive nodded. "As a matter of fact I did and Isabella Hallingbury who saw you at the inn, Belinda. She thought you were running away with the family silver."

"Miss Hallingbury is a fool, and she's spiteful," Belinda said, "but what has that dandy to do with it?"

Mark chuckled. "I had to make up a story so I told him you were an heiress and we were making a runaway match."

Belinda was incensed. "You odious creature! You let him think I was a scheming woman and a rich marriage prize? And he's a gossip? That's the end of my reputation."

Mark was amused by Belinda's fury. "I never used your full name, sweetheart, so he can't say who it was. Stop being coy, Belinda: you know you want to marry me. Clive can take you home and Yardley can lock me up: he won't be able to keep me a prisoner for long."

Clive stepped up to his brother. His expression was so wrathful that Belinda thought he was going to hit Mark.

"Yes, I am going to take Belinda home. She will not marry you for the simple reason that she is going to marry me! And she will marry me because I love her, not to save you or the family honour. You should be horse-whipped for the way you've treated her, making a May-game of her, dragging her round the country and sullying her reputation."

Belinda stood as if turned to stone, she wasn't sure if she had heard right. Her heart fluttered and her knees felt weak.

Yardley was tired of talk, the evening was not turning out at all the way he had expected.

"Take the prisoner to the lock-up in the next village so the magistrate can examine him in the morning. You can take Miss Farrington back to Park Place," he said grudgingly to Clive, "but she mustn't leave the county. She must give evidence at your brother's trial."

"I think not," said Clive. "By then she'll be married to me and Mark will be her brother so her evidence will not be acceptable."

For one glorious moment, Belinda had believed that Clive loved her and truly wanted to marry her but now, with a sinking heart, she realised what Clive was about: marriage to her was merely another way of saving Mark. She stood disconsolate while arrangements were made for one of Yardley's men to take the barouche back to Park Place.

Mark was quite unconcerned. He was marched off calling, "Clive—Belinda, I wish you happy."

Finally, Yardley and his men rode away leaving Belinda and Clive alone at the roadside.

Clive looked down at her and smiled.

Belinda burst into tears and threw herself into his arms. She had had an exhausting day: that morning she had seen the body of the informer and realised the full horror of smuggling; she had danced her first waltz and fallen deeper in love with Clive than ever before, only to discover the contraband in the cupboard that made her certain he was the Master-smuggler. She had tried to warn him and had confided in Mark. She had discovered Mark was unscrupulous and a flirt and then had come the dreadful shock of finding he was the Master-smuggler.

She had been on a madcap journey with heart stopping contretemps; she had been arrested and received proposals of marriage made from expediency not love. Above all, her faith in herself was destroyed. She had realised that every deduction she had made since she came to Suffolk had been wrong. Papa had been right: jumping to hasty conclusions was her besetting sin and it had landed her in dire trouble. No wonder she gave way to a storm of weeping against Clive's chest.

Clive did not know the reason for her tears, but he let her cry, holding her gently but firmly, while stroking her hair. If she could have believed this was affection not comfort, her tears would have dried at once for his touch thrilled her and the nearness of him was making her dizzy.

After a while, her tears abated and she tried to pull herself together. Clive produced a soft white handkerchief and helped her dry her eyes.

She hiccoughed and said, "This has been the most terrible day of my life!"

Clive smiled. "Surely not: three men wanting to marry you—most young women would be in raptures."

"Be serious, sir, the offers meant nothing. What's more important is the terrible wrong I did you in thinking you were the Master-smuggler. Every single judgement I have made has been flawed and I compounded my folly by allowing Mr. Mark to persuade me to help him. I did it for the best of reasons, wanting to save the Sheldons from scandal, but I failed and now he is in prison."

Clive's arm was still round her and he gave her a little squeeze.

"You are too hard on yourself. You helped Mark because of

your goodness of heart and loyalty to my family. I told you once before that to strive and deserve success was almost as good as achieving it."

Belinda shook her head determined to complete her self-abasement.

"Deserve success? Indeed I do not. You don't know the smallpox story." She told him and was surprised when he burst out laughing.

"Oh Belinda, Belinda."

"What will become of Mark?"

"I hope he'll have a good fright. His smuggling escapades have been dangerous and irresponsible, more the sort of thing I would expect from hey-go-mad boys like Will and Simon. He should have grown out of playing with fire by now."

"But the disgrace: your family will be ruined."

"That, my darling, is another wrong conclusion: smuggling is more a peccadillo than a crime in Suffolk."

"What about your parents? They will certainly be upset."

He shook his head. "I think not. Haven't you noticed how philosophical Mamma is about her children's wild ways? Papa won't fuss. He may scowl a bit and scold, but that's all. And Mark will be all right: his godfather is Sir Piers Elsdon, the local magistrate. Sir Piers thinks Yardley's a fool so Papa will easily persuade him not to press charges. This month Mark takes ship for India where he can no longer do any harm."

"But will that satisfy Yardley? He is quite relentless in his pursuit of smugglers and is ambitious to break the ring."

"He'll have to be guided by the magistrate and there'll be other inducements."

"Not a bribe," Belinda said quickly, "you mustn't offer him money, that would make matters worse. Mark tells me Yardley is incorruptible. It's because his father is a merchant whose trade is being spoiled that he is so adamant."

Clive looked at her thoughtfully. "No, I didn't have a bribe in mind—promotion, perhaps and a move to a different area. You seem to know a lot about his affairs. Were you interested in his offer?"

"Most certainly not!" Belinda was indignant. "I don't like him at all and his manner was far too encroaching."

Clive smiled at her vehemence. "What about Mark's offer? Do you care for him?"

Belinda was scornful. "Mark is charming but shallow. He no more wants to marry me than you do."

"That's where you are wrong. My offer was sincere. Didn't you hear what I said, Belinda? I want to marry you for the very good reason that I have fallen in love with you."

Even now, Belinda couldn't believe it. "How could you do so? I am your sisters' governess. I have very little money and I have proved myself to be what you said at the beginning: hen-witted and so irresponsible as to be in need of a governess myself."

In the light from the stars and the tiny crescent moon she could see his loving smile. "Did I say that? How unmannerly of me. I see I shall have to prove to you that I really do love you." Smoothly he enfolded her in his arms and leaned down to kiss her.

Belinda was overwhelmed by the feelings that coursed through her at the touch of his lips: it was more exciting than anything she had ever known. The kiss went on for a long while and she did not ever want it to stop.

When at last he drew back, Clive said, "Oh Belinda, I've wanted to do that many a time." His voice was a little unsteady.

Belinda was almost carried away by the romance of it all but she had to be practical. "Dear Clive, we cannot possibly marry."

He frowned. "Do you not want to marry me? Would it be so disagreeable?"

"How can you ask? But I find it hard to believe you want to share your life with a hen-witted governess."

He grinned and hugged her again. "Am I never to be forgiven for that ill-advised remark? I need you Belinda.

You're so deliciously unpredictable. I need someone who will climb ladders and peer into my window, climb trees from which I am required to extricate her. I need someone who, having cast me as a dastardly villain yet has such kindness and loyalty that she will warn me of imminent arrest. I need someone to rescue trapped dogs without fussing about blood on her dress, who will try to stop a fight she thinks is wrong even if it results in a black eye, someone who will need to be retrieved from a dog's bath. In short, I need someone who will fill my life with surprises and that person, dearest Belinda, must be you!"

"But Clive," Belinda began.

"Hush, my darling," he said. "I will not hear another word against the woman I have chosen to be my wife."

Once again he took her in his arms in masterful fashion and stopped her arguing in the most delightful way with a kiss even more passionate and satisfying than the first.

Belinda revelled in it. This was no longer the worst day of her life but the best. Her heart was filled with joy and happiness. She was certain that this time her judgement was right: Clive Sheldon was the man for her. She wanted to stay in his arms forever.

~ **The End** ~

About the Author

Since her childhood Pamela's loves have been reading, writing and history. She has been a journalist, literary agent, author, teacher of writing and of history, wife and mother. She lives in the country in Norfolk, England with her husband and dogs. When she isn't writing, reading or teaching, she embroiders and cooks. Housework she does not like! She has written several non-fiction books for children and adults and many short stories. Her current love is romance. Her Regency romance 'The Reluctant Governess' is available from Awe-Struck, 'Enchanted Valley', a time-slip serial, is on the net at www.dream-lover.com. She is currently working on a historical romance set during the English Civil War. Her 'Writing a Children's Book' from How To Books is now in its 3rd edition and has been widely praised.